# BIRD, BLOOD, SNOW

*for Dad, for books in the first place*

# CYNAN JONES

# BIRD, BLOOD, SNOW

NEW STORIES FROM THE
# MABINOGION

# SEREN

Seren is the book imprint of
Poetry Wales Press Ltd
57 Nolton Street, Bridgend, Wales, CF31 3AE
www.seren-books.com

© Cynan Jones 2012

ISBN 978-1-85411-589-8

The right of Cynan Jones to be identified as the author of
this work has been asserted in accordance with the Copyright,
Designs and Patents Act, 1988.

A CIP record for this title is available from the British Library.

This book is a work of fiction. The characters and incidents
portrayed are the work of the author's imagination. Any other
resemblance to actual persons, living or dead, is entirely coinci-
dental.

Cover design by Mathew Bevan

Inner design and typesetting by books@lloydrobson.com

Mind map rendered by james@gigantic-design.com

With thanks to the estate of John Steinbeck (*The Acts of King
Arthur and His Noble Knights*, John Steinbeck, Penguin, 2001)

Newspaper article p193 with thanks to the *Cambrian News*

Printed in the Czech Republic by Akcent Media

The publisher acknowledges the financial support of the
Welsh Books Council.

# Contents

# New Stories from the Mabinogion

## Introduction

Some stories, it seems, just keep on going. Whatever you do to them, the words are still whispered abroad, a whistle in the reeds, a bird's song in your ear.

Every culture has its myths; many share ingredients with each other. Stir the pot, retell the tale and you draw out something new, a new flavour, a new meaning maybe. There's no one right version. Perhaps it's because myths were a way of describing our place in the world, of putting people and their search for meaning in a bigger picture that they linger in our imagination.

The eleven stories of the *Mabinogion* ('story of youth') are diverse native Welsh tales taken from two medieval manuscripts. But their roots go back hundreds of years, through written fragments and the unwritten, storytelling tradition. They were first collected under this title, and translated into English, in the nineteenth century.

The *Mabinogion* brings us Celtic mythology, Arthurian romance, and a history of the Island of Britain seen through the eyes of medieval Wales – but tells tales that stretch way beyond the boundaries of contemporary Wales, just as the 'Welsh' part of this island once did: Welsh was once spoken as far north as Edinburgh. In one tale, the gigantic Bendigeidfran wears the crown of London, and his severed head is buried there, facing France, to protect the land from invaders.

There is enchantment and shape-shifting, conflict, peacemaking, love, betrayal. A wife conjured out of flowers is punished for unfaithfulness by being turned into an owl, Arthur and his knights chase a magical wild boar and its piglets from Ireland across south Wales to Cornwall, a prince changes places with the king of the underworld for a year...

Many of these myths are familiar in Wales, and some have filtered through into the wider British tradition, but others are little known beyond the Welsh border. In this series of New Stories from the Mabinogion the old tales are at the heart of the new, to be enjoyed wherever they are read.

Each author has chosen a story to reinvent and retell for their own reasons and in their own way: creating fresh, contemporary tales that speak to us as much of the world we know now as of times long gone.

Penny Thomas, series editor

To my editor,

This is all I have. The police have asked for everything.

I have made copies and transcripts of the material so far. The police records, Peredur's testimonies, the tapes and interviews and medical case notes. In most cases I have removed my questions from the interviews to make things clearer. There are also some press clippings.

You will see where I've started to write things up. It should give you some idea of the approach I intend to take, though it's not quite there yet. The rest of the material I've just tried to slot in at the right point, so at least you have the key events. You will have to feel your way through it instinctively for now.

There is also stuff from _____'s unfinished manuscript. It's drivel. He has hijacked Peredur, tried to mythologise him. I've brought some of his many footnotes [bracketed] into the text to make things easier for you.

I should never have had a lot of this material, but so be it. The police will see that through. There is an implication I am partly responsible for what has just happened. That talking with me brought it all about again. I hope this is not the case. I question, though, whether we are doing the right thing, dramatising this. In the words of one of his doctors:

He shouldn't be romanticised, he shouldn't be revered. It's all very well claiming he was a product of his environment, but we all are. He was a time bomb. And he had so many dead switches that any attempt to defuse him was always doomed to failure. Eventually he was going to go off. Big style.

## A LETTER

Well, I guess time was against us. What do you think? Is there enough here to make something of? This is everything I've accumulated so far. I doubt they will let anyone see him after what he has done now.

Do let me know what you think.

Yours,

--------

...all look distant from behind this glass.

I look down at the sprinkled shards of the skylight, at the black canister that's come through it, up at the outside light.

The black canister perches there, hard against the bright white of the floor, her starched uniform and the red drops of blood.

I do not acknowledge the others coming now, their vain attempts at me.

I look down at the black canister, strange bird bust through that window, and at the white ground and at the red blood, thinking of the woman that time, the bird dead in the snow. And the canister spits. A sharp snake of gas. A smoke.

I told them not to touch my cups. Just don't touch my cups.

# Bird, Blood, Snow

After he'd seen the children he fetched his bike and brought it out into the yard. And then he set about upholstering it.

The children had come into the place on their bikes and they were a great vision to him. Never before had he seen such things.

Their bikes sparkled. The tyres were studded with blocks of rubber and the spokes adorned with dazzling reflectors. The struts of the beautifully painted bikes were aglitter with silver and gold stickers. The pedals and grips were of bold colours, and the saddles plush with pad. They were most proud things.

The children themselves were adorned. Upon their knees and arms they wore bright pads. Their shirts were of vibrant design and on their feet they wore white trainers proud with ticks of gold and silver. The tongues of their trainers were rich and plump and stuck up from the shoe. With their helmets and visors and goggles, their heads were magnificent contraptions.

The boy had pointed at these things and asked what everything was and when they had left he had determined to follow them. He did not recognise their mirth and disbelievement.

When he told his mother that he wished to follow and to play with the children she sat down heavily in a chair. 'No,' she said. Her hands shook as she took another drink, and he went outside. Sometimes his mother was like this.

He brought his bike out into the yard. It was grey and parts of it were rusted, and in some places the rust had lifted the paint. It was run through with bubbling scars. The chrome was mistled. Great chunks were missing from the saddle and it had been wrapped with tape.

The boy took a cloth and washed the bike and soon he believed the grey to be bright silver, and the rust a rosy bronze. The tape he thought the finest leather.

He broke a bottle from the long row outside the door and taped the glass amongst the spokes and the tyres he blackened with creosote. He peeled the labels from rubbish and stuck them to the bike and upon the stabilisers, and upon the plastic saddle box, and so it was made glorious.

He went into the shed and looked among the boxes of his brothers' things. They were not with him now, his older brothers. He had been brought out here to be apart from them.

In the boxes he found shin pads and strapped them to his legs. And he found bright orange swimming bands.

He changed into his most favourite t-shirt and put the crinkly swimming bands over his arms. Then he put a tin bowl on his head.

When he set off his mother came to the door. In his hand he had a sharpened holly stick that was his knife and he began to pedal out of the yard.

The creosote on the tyres left a tar line across the cracked ground and the smell of it came up richly. The grit spat and scattered under the bike, and his mother began to shout: 'That's right, go then! Go and find your father's sort. Oh! They're real men. So kind. So brave.

'You'd better pray you can handle yourself.

'Here's some advice! For out there. Take what you want. Food! Drink! Women. (She laughs.) Steal it all. Be like him.

'Why don't you bring me something back? That will make it all alright. That will make me love you!

'Go on then. Go and be a big man.'

A wailing harangue. He heard her tone turn with sarcasm, but all he gathered from what she said, with the rattle of the wheels, the clatter of stabilisers, the squeak of the chain, through the tin bowl on his head was, misheard, the first part: 'That's right, go then. Go and find Arthur's court.'

He had his mother's blessing.

The children of the estates were divided into groups and they were militarised. Their technology was medieval. They fought with scrap bits of metal and with sticks and stones and it was a wonder there were not more maimings.

The area beyond the estates was a waste forest. Factories had been taken down, warehouses cleared. In the ground, railways grew over disused, like ancient forest tracks.

Behind the land were the mountains, and it was as if the vegetation and wildness of them had made raid on this waste ground.

In the more open spaces and the old industrial yards dandelions and buddleia grew, and willowherb had taken hold. Other places were thick with sallow.

To a man this was a distraught place, but to a child this was a territory.

NOTE: As I understand it, the boy's mother took

him from these estates to try to keep him out of trouble.

His father made a living from crime and violence and had paid the price for that. His older brothers too.

Peredur was the youngest son (of seven) and she did not want him ending up the same way.

Seemingly she came to some arrangement with the owners of a nearby holiday retirement village and they moved into the run-down pre-fab that used to be part of the old farm where the holiday village was sited.

It was a collection of lodges on tidy grounds, each served by its own garden. The only people around were meek old men and women who gave the boy no notion that such things as battles and weapons existed, and he spent his days playing among the cabins and the well-kept lawns. He could have been a sweet child.

*What do you remember of it?*

*A glittering. The wires glittering…*

*…a throb in the earth.*

# BIRD, BLOOD, SNOW

*It is a growl, a thick hum. A bark of dogs. Winter. And he stands. Night time. A sad moon.*

*He is not yet subject to myths of fright, an innocent.*

*He stands before the high wire panels at the boundary of the village, watches the moonlight hit and travel in the mesh.*

*And the deer hits. Like the sound of broken bottles. Buckles and he sees its flank pattern into the wire a guttural scream and bright lights come with the thwack of snapped sticks the silhouette of men. In the air around him the summery whizz of flies tracing out from the white lights and the dogs come, as the doe drops from the fence screams at its torn meat and the mesh comes alive, a tension in the metal, sparks, lights, with electricity.*

*Poor deer. Poor deer. Peredur.*

*Were you frightened?*

*I was spellbound.*

Imagine how she felt when she saw him. The Wendy house sat up on decking and looked from the end of the neat garden out over the fields around and he rode up.

The doors of the Wendy house were open and there was a plastic yellow chair near the doorway and in the chair sat the pretty auburn-haired girl. She was dressed up as a princess.

About her forehead was a golden crown of plastic, studded with fake jewels, and she wore a thick gold ring of the same on her hand. On the floor of the Wendy house were books of fairy tales.

Peredur was very hungry by now for he had been riding for some time. He dismounted from his bike and approached the girl. She asked him if he wished to play.

Inside the Wendy house there was a table with a jug of squash and some mini sausage rolls. The girl thought that Peredur must be on a quest, for she was well acquainted with stories of chivalrous knights and crusaders.

'Are you a knight in shining armour?' she asked.

The boy had never played with other children before and did not understand. So she showed him the books, and the pictures of the knights jousting and winning trials of combat.

He said he was hungry, and the girl bade him take some food. He saw the gold ring upon her finger and asked for it.

'Take it,' she said, for she knew from the stories that it was right to give such a trinket to a brave knight as a token of her blessing. She giggled as he took the plastic ring off from her finger, and closed her eyes, waiting. Nothing came. She waited for his kiss.

When she opened her eyes he had taken another handful of sausage rolls and was walking off. The shin pads were too big and slapped against his legs.

When her father came into the Wendy house he was furious. He could see the tracks of the bike and of the lines of creosote marking the new decking.

'Tell me,' he said to the girl, 'who has been here since I left you?'

'Just a boy,' the girl said. 'He was dressed up all odd. We played knights and princesses.'

'Did he touch you?' asked the father. The girl did not understand. 'Did he do anything to you?' he asked again, and she shook her head, and she still did not understand.

'I don't believe you,' her father said. He felt sick inside. He felt dizzy looking at the black tyre marks.

'Get inside.' And he banished the girl then from the Wendy house.

The smell of the fire travelled on the wind and in it you could smell the things they burned.

The gang sat around the fire and now and again attended it. They sat on tubs and bricks they had collected from about the distraught place. It was a demolished warehouse site and buddleia came up through the cracked concrete floor. Much of the brick that remained had begun to crumble and the lines of the walls were still visible. In some places they were a foot or so high. In that way, the space was something like a courtyard.

The gang shied when the older boy came up to them. He was a few years older. He let his bike drop to the ground and walked up to them. Under his cap his head was shaven with a pattern. One of the girls there muttered under her breath.

The older boy demanded that they share their drink with him. He grabbed the vodka bottle from the girl. The boastful talk amongst them had stopped.

The older boy took a swig from the bottle and looked down at the gang. Each of them seemed to shrink. The girl who had muttered pulled her top around her and looked away. She had gone very red and the boy grinned down at her. He spat into the fire and the alcohol flamed up and showed the red in her face even more. He kicked a few things closer into the fire.

There was broken glass about and on the one remaining higher wall was colourful graffiti. Something split in the fire.

'Ignoring me, now, hey?' he said. 'Fuck off,' she said, under her breath.

He splashed the vodka at her and when she jerked up in surprise he struck her round the ear. The vodka was down her face and her top had fallen open again and the drink fell down onto her chest. Her ear reddened. The gang shrank.

'Don't want this back?' he said. He poured the vodka very slowly out onto the ground.

'Not going to stand up for her?' The tears and the strong alcohol stung the girl's eyes. 'Pah!'

The older boy picked up his bike. 'Come and get it,' he said, and he rode out of the courtyard to the old car park, sitting very low back on his bike, riding with one hand, swigging the vodka in his other.

The gang hung their heads and didn't look at each other. The older boy was much bigger. Something cracked in the fire again.

Thereupon, Peredur came into the courtyard on his old grey bike. He saw the proud, well-attired gang around the fire and rode up to them.

One of the taller boys, Kay, stood up. He was drunk from the vodka and he was drunk from the humiliation of the older boy.

'Are you Arthur's lot?' Peredur asked.

'What do you want with Arthur's lot?' Kay asked. He wanted to beat down on the ridiculous boy.

The gang could not believe the look of him. His tin bowl was still upon his head and he looked ridiculous. They began to make fun of him and to throw sticks at him. They tried to forget the older boy.

There were two younger children with the gang, a short girl and her brother. Their clothes were partly wet where they'd come off their bike fetching sweets for the gang and they were drying on them in front of the fire.

The big circle around the fire was an ashy slake and it was full with nails from the burned palettes and boxes, and glass that had bubbled in the heat.

'Are you a hero or something?' asked the little boy.

This angered the drunk Kay, and he struck the child. 'What? You think *he's* some hero?'

'He's cool dressed up like that,' the little girl said. She was picking out nails that had rusted almost to wires in the fire. And again Kay pushed her down so she cut her hands on the sweets of glass.

Peredur did not understand the tall boy's behaviour but an instinct flared in him. He remembered how he had been treated before moving off the estate. He felt a strange and basic protectiveness.

'Where's Arthur?' said Peredur.

'What?' said Kay. The gang felt bigger in themselves again now. 'Go and get our voddie back.'

He pointed out the older boy who was still riding his bike in the old car park.

'Go and get that bottle off him and you can join our gang.'

'Ok,' Peredur said. And he wheeled his bike round and went out. They laughed as he went.

When he arrived the older boy was standing upright on the pedals of his bike hopping it in circles while he swigged at the bottle. He sat and pulled the bike into a wheelie as he came towards the boy and threw down the empty bottle into the grass.

'They all too chicken?'

The older boy sat astride his bike, sitting low back, his baggy tracksuit shiny about him. Under the peak of his cap there were two strips shaved into his eyebrow.

'They told me to come and get their bottle back.'

Peredur stood there in his favourite t-shirt and the wrinkled armbands and the shin pads on his legs and the tin bowl that didn't fit properly on his head.

'Whatever! Just go and tell them to come and get

it. They're taking the piss.'

The place was like a distraught meadow. The tarmac of the parking bays had been scraped up and grass had crept its way back. Here and there a willow burst from the ground. Piled earth and spoil made small mounds that were cut up with bike tracks. The boy went to pick the bottle up. This incensed the youth.

He scooted up on his bike, walking it along, and slipped off the grip from his handlebar and with the butt of the grip struck Peredur firmly between his shoulder and his neck. There was a brief hesitation when Peredur hardly moved. Then something snapped.

He had never before been struck. Not once had a hand been raised to him in direct violence. He did not understand the act.

*But there was something there. Yes. Some distant bark inside my blood. My chemicals collided. I felt extremely calm. The light caught the bottle in the grass and it looked like some strange kind of water. The dull throb ached out from my neck, more like sun falling on a part of my body than anything. I kind of felt a warm, lazy calmness. I turned around and pushed him. I think he was surprised.*

*He fell over his bike, clumsy, and I hopped onto him and then I looked at the two stripes shaved into his eyebrow as a kind of sighting line and lifted up my arm with the holly stick. Easy. Like a stretch in my sleep.*

He span round and pushed the older boy and, only half on the bike as he was, he fell awkwardly. The small child lit up. His surprise and spitting fury made the older boy laugh, a yawing delinquent clamorous laugh that split suddenly into a wheeling muffled scream, a scream already blocked with fluid as the dart smashed through his eye and out through the nape of his neck. He lay there, gasping like fish, his blood bubbling and oozing.

'That was tight,' Owain said to Kay. 'You shouldn't have sent him. He's obviously not right. It makes us look like we're taking the piss. What if he's got brothers or something?

'I bet he's had a beating.'

He got up to go and see what had happened and made his way to the old car park.

When he arrived Peredur was dragging the older boy behind him along the ground.

'There's your bottle,' he said. 'Tell Arthur I did this. And tell that tall one he should be careful picking on those little ones.'

When Owain got back to the gang he was white pale and had been sick. He still shook.

'He didn't want to be in the gang,' he said.

From *The Celtic Echo*

## Child Terror

### Local Youths 'Afraid To Go Out'

Local youths have been terrorised by a one-boy crime wave. The boy, who can't be named owing to his young age, is said to be making the other children and teenagers 'afraid to go out'.

So far there have been sixteen reports of violent acts against other youths, and many other complaints, including the intimidation of a young girl in her own garden and the theft of some cake.

'I know the kids are no saints themselves,' says local parent Roy Hobbs, 'but this one is beyond. He is something else.' Mr Hobbs of Cwrt y Brenin called police after his son, 16, came home with a 10" piece of holly stick through his new bicycle helmet.

'He's going around with a big stick and it's bullying. There's no other word for it.'

We spoke to one boy who didn't want to be named for fear of revenge.

'You are just playing around on your bike with your mates, doing wheelies and ramps and stuff and he just comes out of nowhere carrying this long pole and charges you and if you are unlucky he knocks you off your bike,' he said.

When asked why they didn't do something to stop the child, the boy said, 'We would get into trouble. Also, he is quite scary.'

A police spokesman said, 'Several youths between the ages of about eleven and sixteen have been driven over their bike saddles to the ground and there have been a number of other injuries and some damage to bikes and clothes.'

When asked what police were doing about the rogue youngster, he said, 'We are trying to locate the child. We have spoken with his mother who said he disappeared a week ago. At the same time, because he has committed crimes and is not simply missing but subject to a criminal investigation, we have to protect his identity as he is so young. So it is difficult. The parents are very angry and we also have to protect the child from possible illegal retribution.'

And the father of the young girl whose cake was stolen had no hesitation telling us: 'If I get my hands on him I will teach him a lesson. I am very proud of my little girl and still don't believe that all he did was pinch her cake. Anything could have happened.' It is also clear that the boy took a plastic ring from the girl.

The plot thickened when on further investigation our reporter uncovered that several child gangs were operating in the area. Local Child Welfare Officer Nikki Hollis said she was aware of the gangs.

'They are generally a mix of older and younger children – both boys and girls – and are generally defined by where the young people come from on the estates. Young people are keen to feel they belong to something and these gangs are an inevitable part of growing up here. Obviously this new boy has come in from outside.'

Talking to older gang members, who preferred to remain anonymous, our reporter was horrified to be told of 'large stashes of weapons' ranging from sticks and stones to catapults, home-made crossbows and bits of pipe.

'Whoever controls the technology controls the estates,' said one gang leader. 'The better weapons you can make or get hold of, the more powerful you are. But this kid has no fear. He will come at you with a stick.'

When asked whether they were aware of these gangs, one parent said, 'I know the kids split into gangs and fights do happen. But that's natural. There is nothing for the children to do here so they end up fighting, but until now it's all been high jinx.'

The fights are often organised and some have been filmed on mobile phones and put up on youtube.

One concerned resident said, 'Maybe this is what these kids need. It might sort them out.'

For legal reasons the details cannot be published

but we can reveal that the boy allegedly responsible for these crimes was born on one of the estates but was taken away by his mother at a young age. We spoke to an ex-neighbour, Mr Sikes, 72, who remembers the child: '(He) was an ugly little thing, all shrivelled it seemed to me. He was ill-tempered, always wailing and generally frightful. He would bite and hit. He was a terror to his poor mother.'

Rev Edmund Jones, local minister, also remembers the baby: 'I saw him myself. There was something diabolical in the way he looked, the way he moved. He screamed all the time, which used to frighten people, but otherwise he was harmless.'

It is also thought that the boy might be responsible for the grievous assault last Sunday on a sixteen year old who was beaten to the ground and stabbed in the eye with a sharpened stick. There were no eye witnesses. The boy is still in hospital in critical condition.

# BIRD, BLOOD, SNOW

*A functional room in the police station. Daytime. Various information posters on the walls, most of them somewhat torn. A big whiteboard. They sit round an unfussy table.*

– Sixteen counts of ABH. (*Shuffles the papers.*) That's not including that boy he turned into a vegetable. (*Takes a swig of coffee, clearly it's luke- warm.*) In his fucking eye! Christ!

– "No-eye" witnesses. I can't believe they wrote that. (*A snigger.*) So what's the story?

– Mother, alcoholic. Father, deceased. Tits up in the boating lake. Never knew a duck would go for something's face like that. Wasn't pretty. Probable a water rat or something got at it first. I don't think the duck knew what it was doing.

– (*Shuffles papers, fingers the lines of information.*) ...brother, one – no, three. Half-brothers they are, I should say – arrested. Another deceased. Two others AWOL. Warrants out...

– Quite a tribe, then.

– Quite a tribe. Fair dos, she tried to get him out of that. Third wife, incidentally. I say wife. Not *actual* wife. Nineteen when she had the boy, which made him Ap Efrog boy number seven. All accounts she upped and left.

– To?

– Seems she had some kind of *arrangement* with the guys running the retirement village. Apparently she's their on-site cleaner. I guess they owed Efrog a favour. From what I've heard, she's away with the fairies.

– Those cabins?

– Those cabins.

– And now?

– Still there.

– (*In a sappy voice, all sorry sounding.*) But her kid's all growed up.

– All growed up. Oh well. At least he's livened things up a bit. We were in need of some entertainment ...what do you do with a fucking eight year old who sticks a fucking stick in someone's eye?

– Social Services.

– Social Services. They're already talking to her. Fat lot of use that will do. (*Pauses. He fingers the case sheets. Looks momentarily grim.*) You should read these.

*They look up at a monitor, at the eight year old sitting quietly on the bed in the holding room and looking innocent and like he wouldn't say boo to a goose.*

– We need to go and speak to his mother again.

The police pulled up in the yard and got out of the car.

– We should have a WPC with us, one said. They looked at the dilapidation of the place.

They knocked a lot before she let them in and she came to the door in a shift with an old worn jumper over it. The younger of the policeman felt slightly sick at the sight. For some reason he thought of a dead gull floating at the edge of a pond.

– Mrs Efrog, said the other policeman.

– Don't use that name now, she spat. There was a hesitation.

– May we come in?

They went into the lounge and she went back into the chair like she was sucked back into it. The younger policeman didn't want to sit down in the place. Everywhere there were black sacks of clothes that had never been unpacked.

The air was not shifting in the room and the place was thick with cigarette smoke and stank artificially of the plug-in room scenter. The telly was on with the sound off.

– We've found your son, they said.

There was a horrible moment when she seemed to solidify, as if her mind went from a thick gloopy paste to a grey crust like before you get sick. Then she spoke.

– He was such a nice boy. Such a nice boy.

That cloud of blue smoke hung there like a separate atmosphere.

The younger policeman was looking at a strange

sick-looking stain on the carpet and he had no idea what it was.

She started to talk of her son. The young policeman phased out. He couldn't connect. His eye went over the room. Shreds of carpet were up where it met the door to the kitchen and it looked like a hide torn up, the netted plastic beneath a grey weave like the sheath over a muscle. He couldn't shake the idea of dead animals out of his head. The lino the other side of the carpet grip in the door was worn so that there were big scales in the pattern. It was filthy. You could see that from here.

He stared at the bright gold carpet grip, lined and patterned like some fabulous artefact.

– He is a shepherd, my boy. A shepherd.

– Mrs Ef... you are aware it's your son, probably, committing these assaults.

The younger policeman was staring at one of the black sacks. It had split and the extraordinarily coloured shoe had come out of it, as if it had hatched itself onto the carpet.

– My little goats he used to call them. My little goats. Such a gentle boy.

*There was an ammonial smell as he lifted the log and the boy squatted back, sitting on his heels. A rich smell too came up off the leaf litter. Had you seen the log, you would have thought the boy too young to lift it. But he had unusual strength.*

*He watched the woodlice scatter, the boy, now and then herding them again into the centre of the log with the end of his stick.*

*He was too young to count very far, but made a show of it, tallying off the grey woodlice as he always did. His numbers were his own, and it was the process of tallying that was the thing.*

*Presently the woodlice ceased to scatter and they gathered as a herd. He stroked their backs and they crouched and stilled.*

*When he went back to the log that next day and raised*

*it again, he saw the earwigs there amongst the woodlice. He was concerned that they were some horrible outcasts. They were foreign and unusual to him and he marvelled at them, thinking that they must have been missing for a long time, running wild under the trees, so thin and undernourished they seemed compared to the others.*

*Driving them and steering them, he succeeded in catching both in his hands, and ran to his mother.*

*'I found a strange thing, Mam,' he said, and he opened his fist.*

*'My!' said his mother, 'you must have been as fast as St Shane to catch them,' and she beamed, for she was sober then, and okay with the world.*

– Come on, he said. We're getting nowhere here.

The woman was absent. It was as if she slept with her eyes open. Some small change happened in the light outside, and for a moment the bottles that were about the floor seemed to enlarge, as if they had taken a breath.

– You realise that it's likely your son will be taken
    into foster care, said the policeman.

She looked at him then. Her jaw slipped like it was
gaining weight.

No, she said. No.

Peredur had gone from there, leaving the youth bleeding out into the grass of the old lot.

He remembered the pictures in the little girl's books.

When he met the other boy he stopped his bike. There was a moment of utter derision from the other boy, seeing how he looked.

'You with them lot from Cwrt y Brenin?' he asked Peredur.

'I am with Arthur,' Peredur said.

'I wouldn't admit that if I was you,' said the other, older boy.

'I am looking for Arthur,' Peredur said.

The other boy did not know what he meant by that.

'Well, if you're from Cwrt y Brenin that means I don't have much choice. Can't just let you pass. Rules are rules.'

Peredur looked around at the edgeland of the place. A large patch of burdock grew close by with a kind of regal aspect. He stared at a patch of scarlet cups, a strange fungus there by his feet. He seemed to see everything in hyper-detail.

When he got off the boy he picked up the half block and stood over him.

'You tell him,' he said, 'I did this because you made me.'

The other boy's hand was in the air, stretched before him, his fingers spread wide, as if he would be able to catch the block. He was frightened.

'I'll tell them,' he said. He had wet himself. He had felt that Peredur had beaten him with stones.

Peredur watched him cycle away. He looked up. The clouds were moving passively over. He felt an affinity. Their calm, distant flight.

# CYNAN JONES

From *The Celtic Echo*

Correction: In last week's article 'Child Terror' we erroneously reported the child had stolen some cake. It was in fact mini sausage rolls. We apologise for any confusion the error might have caused.

From that time on I have felt that I am not always in my right mind, and my reason is sometimes all over the place, and I have done a thousand mad acts.

I was seen by a number of people. [*Note: find Ed. Psych reports, dossier from fostering agency.*] Most of the questions were ridiculous.

  – Show me on the doll where your father touched you. Point to cock.

  – What is your favourite colour? Red.

  – Why? The colour of blood. Blah, blah.

The foster family was paid very well. I was considered disruptive. He took time off work to 'protect his family' from me and was compensated for that.

As I said, I saw a number of people, and they decided I should be 'Kept Occupied'. I call them 'they'. They had various ideas. Fishing (calm) and woodwork (constructive). And boxing (an 'outlet').

The gym had this smell to it. There was an old cabinet in the house they'd taken me from like that. Layers of use and varnish. It stank alternately of sweat and Lynx; and sometimes someone would bring in a chip supper, watch the bouts. That would stink the place out.

I would get taxis everywhere because they paid for everything. When they dropped me off at the door the old guy was having a cigarette outside. He went in and I followed him. I noticed he had a limp.

It didn't feel it to me back then but it was a small place. What was I? Eight? Nine?

First time I went in it was the light got me. Such a white light. Ominous dark windows up around by the ceiling, nothing you could look out of. And the noise. If the footwork was good, the brush of the daps on the canvas. And the speedball, going like a train. Yes, all that. Had quite an impression on me.

I think they called it 'An Outlet For His Anger'. They should have said aggression. I don't think they knew the difference. Whatever. The idea was to 'Calm Me Down'. Right! The idea was to put me up against some bigger kids so I learnt I wasn't so tough. Except that wasn't going to work, was it? You can fight or you can't. Some people who can fight never find it out. Others fight all the time and are never good at it. It's a gift. Something you're given. And when you're little, like I was then compared to the others, you're not going to *half* do it, are you?

Well, I watched the sparring for a while. (Later – that time I had to go through the kitchens to get out of a place, the police piling in at the front – the light, the activity, the noise back there, kind of reminded me again of all this.)

He patted the bench next to him, the old man, and I went and sat down. It had a smell, too, that bench. A smell of leather and the musk of the old man's sweat. And the same smell of wood that was under everything. I was so much smaller than him that I didn't sink at all into the cushion, just rested up on it.

It was out of place there, too grand that bench, embroidered at the back with this tapestry of an old stag hunt. The woven dogs were after the stag and it was twisted and I remembered the deer in the fence. I wondered if all that polished, varnishy smell in the place came out of the bench. There was a weird heat given out by an old coil heater up on the wall. You have to remember it was a few years ago now. Orange wires, glowing there.

'You know how to box?' he asked me.

I guess Uncle, as we called him, was the first person to have *influence* on me. The first *real* person I listened to.

'I suppose,' I said, 'if someone taught me, I would know.'

'If you know how to throw a stone,' he replied, 'you know how to throw a punch.'

There were two lads in the ring, few years older than me, eleven, twelve-ish. They were all padded up;

body pads and gloves, and head guards – one yellow, one a kind of dark red, almost brown, leathery – same as the old bench.

'Tell me,' said the man, 'which of the lads fights better?'

The two coloured, plasticy heads were bobbing round like balls on water. It wasn't like I was used to from the fights I'd got into. There weren't many punches going in.

'The one with the yellow hat,' I said, 'could probably have the other one if he wanted to.'

The old man looked at me. First time I remember anyone doing that. Seemed to last a long time, that look. With a kind of interest if you like. Without some comment coming. Some snigger.

'Go and put some gloves on kid. Have his head guard. See if you can get a hit in on the yellow lad there.'

They put on the gloves for me, weird feeling. Suddenly my hands felt floaty. The head guard was wet with the other kid's sweat. They laced it up warm. It was too big really, and shifted about when they made me shake my head; so they taped it down.

Can't smell glue without thinking of that.

I wonder if 'they' realised the mistake they'd made right away. I don't think he even got a punch off, but I get like that, always have: don't feel a thing against myself once it starts.

I just kept punching him, all in the face, until his eyebrow was down over his eye and the blood was streaming.

Uncle was up on his feet. He was stroking his hand through his grey hair and giving me that look. They were patching up the other kid. Not much use, those head guards. It took no time at all. The blood was coming out so fast it was pooling up against his cheek guard until they took it off.

'Well, boy,' said Uncle. 'Come and sit a minute. You're quite something, aren't you.'

Yes. I am quite something.

I remember when he first turned up at the gym. He was a scrawny thing. Big lumps of bone in him and these kind of elastic muscles. You probably know the name the other kids had for him, behind his back. Kids are cruel and right like that.

He was too young to start really but they pushed for it. They played it down, what he'd done, but the talk was about and I knew. I'd had other kids similar. Not quite like him. But there for the same reason.

I tried to give him something to lose. I tried to give him a sense he had talent, and that if he practised he could be good, and that if he messed up he'd throw all that away.

Born days, I'd never seen anything like it. There was a kind of calm and control. You would not believe the speed. A kid of his age. He made other people look frozen.

'Look,' I told him. 'Everyone's going to tell you you're a bad kid. They're going to pick on you, and push you. What you've got is a big thing, but it can go against you.' I told him he was uncommonly strong. I remember that because I don't think I'd ever said the word 'uncommonly' before. But I didn't want to say unnatural. Unnatural made it sound like he was weird, but uncommon, well, like he was special.

'Whatever they do to wind you up,' I said, 'just take it. Don't react. Don't worry if you don't understand it.' I tried to get him to understand it was all about discipline. 'Trust me,' I said, 'and don't get involved.'

I'm telling it now like it happened right after, but it was a while, a few years maybe – they brought someone in to watch me. Again some old guy, this time with a couple of others with him. I think they were shocked how little I was. Young, I mean.

'So, you know how to punch,' said the man.

There was a big heavy bag in the corner of the hall, probably as big round as I could reach back then.

'Glove up,' said the man, 'let's see you work the bag.'

What happened next is something I swear to. On Halfpenny's leg. Don't ask me to understand it. But sometimes we're given signs.

I went at the bag. It had to weigh forty-five kilos, (I know it did, it was written right there, large, right where I was punching it), and the thing came off the hook. I lifted it up and dropped it off the hook.

There was a kind of consternation.

It took a few of them to hang it back and I went at the bag again. The hook itself came down, little bits of plasterboard and paint, and they couldn't hang it back then. A few punches in, right-hander, that's the truth. The thump of the bag coming down again shut everybody up. I was pretty much as surprised as them.

'Well, lad,' said the guy. He was kind of aglitter now. 'I've never seen a boy punch like that. You've not even started to grow yet. Mercy,' he said, I heard him saying it, 'what this bastard will do when he fills out.'

*– The boxing seemed to help.*

*Yes. I held it together for a while. It was something to focus on.*

*– Where was Arthur at this time?*

*He was there, quietly there.*

*– But you weren't on such a quest.*

*I tried to let things go.*

*That was difficult, sometimes. In school.*

I could take people picking on me and they knew the lines. They didn't push too far. But it was just seeing how anything weak got picked on. Anything weak or different. Even the teachers. How they would 'Make An Example' of somebody. I didn't understand it.

Leave it alone, Uncle had said. Don't get involved.

–You saw yourself as some sort of protector?

I was different, but I was not weak.

I heard crying and there she was, pretty little thing twtied by her bike all tears and sniffles, clutching her Ken. The doll kept coming apart. Its legs and arms and head were ripped off and she kept trying to stick them on, and they would fall to the ground, and then her crying would go up another notch. Why did they push me like this?

I asked 'Why are you crying?'

'Your fault, your fault,' she said. Every time she sniffed the little syrup of snot she had shot back up her nostril, like a snail hiding.

'Why is it my fault?' I said.

'You made your mother die. Because you ran off from her and she died.'

Now, I have to admit to not knowing this. They'd taken me away from her, yes; because she was an 'influence'; but this was the first I'd heard of her death. I can't really remember how that felt. Just that there was a great coming back of something in me.

She kept talking, twtied there over her broken man doll. Something about kids, but my head was like when the wind gets right into the trees and it's all just movement and noise. The loudest hush.

'...and because you live with us,' – she was their natural born child – 'he broke my doll. And he said you'd be next, if you went anywhere near him.'

Well, a great calmness came on me. What's the point in not being what you are? It was like all that rage and sound, the crashing branches in my head, had stilled. Stilled into a great tree waiting to be cut down on something. And somewhere, up there, whispering in its branches, my little voice was back.

I helped her bury the doll, and then I went after him.

From *Police Taped Interview # xxxx Incident No. XX*
Case: _____

'He's a fucking lunatic, man.'

'Ok, ok. Let's calm down.'

'Calm down! Fuck. He's a fucking...'

'Enough. Right. Get him out of here.'

On the tape there is the sound of the chair scrape and the door and the kid being taken out; a shout of 'Hey, watch my arm, man.'

'Fucking kids.'

As you went out from the centre of the town it was like paint had peeled off things with age. The veneer fell away. Each consequent street looked worse.

The big house was at the end of an empty street mostly empty of cars. That made it look not properly inhabited.

The house was covered with scaffold and the state of the scaffolding suggested it had been there some time. The poles were pocked and rusted. The small garden in front had gone feral. Peredur stopped outside the place.

From the scaffolding a bony head looked down on him. The light of the sky behind gave it a fuzz of blond-red hair. A face seemed to spiral down, investigate, recognise the boy as someone like itself. (Did the place choose Peredur, or did Peredur choose the place?)

'You wanting in? Or are you looking for someone?' The voice fell down on Peredur, felt bony, hit him somewhat. Little chippings of words.

He had not eaten, Peredur, and was hungry and faint. All about the cracked paving in front there were the little flags of ash trees.

'Ask can I come in,' Peredur said.

Soon after, the door opened. The floorboards had been taken up in the entrance and there was a walkway made of scaffold planks.

He went through into the front room. Some twenty or so figures lay about. They were difficult to determine in the low light.

The windows were blind squares of chipboard and the air was thick with dope. It stank of piss in the room. From the trappings still around you could see the place had once been an hotel.

They lay about in abstract clothes distraught with individuality. They were all marked some deliberate way, had dyed hair, pictures in their skin, metal in the skins. They looked all the same somehow. They were not functional.

A fire burned in the grate and in the thick heat and the light of it the bodies through the smoke looked like they bobbed in a soup. Peredur felt light headed. [*We don't know, his memory is unclear on this, but he had been without food for several days now.*

*He had dealt with the boy who broke the doll and then gone out into the brake beyond the estates. He felt numb about his mother.*] Bits of the ornate wooden fire surround were pulled off and were burning in the fire.

Suddenly the television volume cracked on. There

was a girl band on the screen, but it was as if she had come from the TV, a chamber she had walked into the room from.

*She was in a ripped silk dress and her skin showed white through the dress.*

His floating eyes lit upon her, went back to the television, his mind following. It was like his mind was a butterfly, blinking, flapping its wings on the flower of the screen.

*I remember her black hair and her red cheeks. On her cheeks she'd painted hearts. She was a deck of cards.*

The butterfly took off, a small fish, fluttered through the soup.

*I had never seen such a beautiful sight.*

'Are you okay? she asked, her voice, her voice herbs sinking in the fluid. [*He was almost certainly ill.*]

Not long after the batteries of the television went two others came in with food. One carried a fat three-litre flagon of cider, the other loaves of bread.

'There was fuck all there. Hot food counter's been cleared out,' he hears one say. 'Why is there a kid in here?'

*She was kind to me. It was like a pure kind. Different from the others.*

Take it, she says, take it. Her face, fallen from the television, floats before him. He chokes, coughs. The image of her scattering, petals collapsing from a dead flower. He tries to hand the bread away. Share it. Share it.

You want more, she says. Take more.

'Sleep,' he says. 'Need sleep.'

He hears her talk, a gentle breeze blowing, that blows about the petals of her face.

She makes a bed of cushions for him, like a mother.

– Sis, think you're kind of sweet on him.

– What?

– Give him some of this.

– Fuck off. No way. He's like a kid.

He was woken by the crashing door as the police came in, the cursing as they missed their footing in the hall.

# BIRD, BLOOD, SNOW

*Memo to Social Services regarding care placement*

re: Peredur Ap Efrog

Recommend moving P. to residential children's home.

Currently recovering in hospital (suffering exposure, dehydration), following removal from squat. Evidence of cannabis in bloodstream but unlikely to have been direct.

Suggest he is moved directly medical staff happy. Clearly placement in foster care not working.

The boy that opened the door was my age but he had the build of a man. When he opened the door it was clear he was simple. There were rabbits on his outsize pyjamas. There was some big woman behind him watching him carefully. It was a special treat for him, being allowed to open the door.

They signed me over and the social worker and the police officer left. I could hear the simple boy being allowed to shut the door behind them. That was as good as it got, for him.

Don't stay. Don't.

None of the others had talked to me but this girl. She was like a small newt girl. A small wet newt. (I remembered, then, the name they used to call me. In a way I quite liked that. It gave me a kind of mythology.) She was detached from the world and her words moved like she was tiny and wet and clambering through grass.

There are nine of them, said the newt. And Mother and Father. I felt her words moving over me like a newt. They won't let us out.

I saw how scared they all were. How timid. They'll let me out, I thought to myself.

I lay awake. Something in my brain was asking to be known. It was like a word you can't quite think of battering around the inside front of your skull as you try to remember it, like a big fat fly against a window.

I watched the light change, coming through the curtains onto the wall before me. The orangey light of the night lamps around the building gave way to a powdery white. Then there was the pattern of the leaves, backlit on the curtain, and I saw pictures in that, and that's when the boy screamed.

I went out into the corridor. The carer was grabbing hold of the boy and he was screaming.

It was surprising how easily her skull split. When I rammed it into the corridor wall. It made a sort of eggy sound, really. Her hair cap spread out like a dish on her head.

She started gibbering. Please. Please. Peredur, please. Skulls bleed, they really do. The blood was spitting when she talked.

She fell to blubbering.

They told me. They told me you'd hurt people. We knew you would hurt someone. You have to let us help you.

I had only been there a night. I was surprised that she knew me. Again I felt that lovely sunshine calmness after busting her. Some odd white liquid ran from her nose.

Later I found out he walked in his sleep. That he did this. That he often screamed at daybreak. Woops!

# BIRD, BLOOD, SNOW

*Rough. Mostly from unfinished MSS, by* _____.

This is how it is told. He had, our gallant hero, stuck it three weeks at the place. Then he gathered what weapons he could [such things as sharpened pencils, marker pens, a dinner knife from the canteen which he sharpened up], took one of the old witches' bikes, and left. [As he would put it, he 'went on his way'. Later the terms 'escaped' and 'broke out' would be used.] He was now eleven years old.

It was Baltic cold. The bike was too much a palfrey and not built for him, and he rode it to dismantlement. Finally the front wheel buckled, and he abandoned the bike in a ditch.

For a while the cold abated, but as dusk dropped so the temperature did. Heroic or not, our hero was cold. [It is likely that this lowered tolerance to the elements was a result of his being kept almost entirely indoors, in a centrally heated, double-glazed environment, for the three weeks of his stay at the home. It is certainly not in keeping with his previous outdoor character.]

It did not occur to him to hitchhike, but the car pulled over anyway. Unaware of the possible repercussions, our hero – taciturn though he was and not best at politeness – accepted a lift. In his mind he saw that Arthur had sent the car to him as a token of his worth.

'Where are you going?' asked our hero's deliverer.

He explained that he had nowhere fixed.

'Then stay with me. I have room.'

And he stayed that night with the hermit.


'Would you like a cup of tea? Orange squash?'

The boy had recoiled. He had felt an unusual instinct when the man ushered him in. The hallway of the bungalow was prim.

He sat on the sofa. There was an electric hearth and the fake coals were warming up, giving out a glow the colour of streetlight, like the orange lamps around the place he had just left.

The boy sat awkwardly on the sofa and felt its very great difference from the old leathered bench in the gym, times back. There was no *real* smell in this place.

'You look cold,' said the man. 'Why don't you kneel in front of the fire?'

In some ways, a degree of uncertainty had been introduced into the boy in the foster home and over the last few weeks and he did not have his previous faith in himself. So he went to kneel before the fire.

On the veneered shelf above the hearth were some pictures of the man himself and some slate mats engraved with landmarks, and in the centre a statue of a triple harp.

At that moment, as if the harp had come alive, a music filled the room. The man seemed to stroke the speaker, and put the remote control down.

He said 'A nice cup of tea,' and went through to the kitchen.

The music affected the boy. It somehow seemed to berate him. The music smiled fakely while it patronised him, as if it – like the witches at the home – were telling him what was best.

He thought about running. He felt distrustful of the place and of the fake hearth. There was a horrible domesticity, the odd air of an environment built too consciously. He was no longer, however, subject simply to his instinct. I guess it's what Arthur wants, he thought. Faith – with the loss of confidence – fills in.

The music kept going. It was clambering and fawning over him. He thought of the newt at the home, felt it pluck with wet fingers at him.

The boy looked through to the kitchen at the man making a cup of tea. There was a corner cupboard and on it a tea set arranged with the teapot there in the centre, everything in its place.

The man took down two cups and made the tea with bags in the cups. He saw the man squeeze the bags against the side of the cups and carry them on the spoon in his clean podgy little hand to a little pot and the boy for some reason felt nervous and a little sick.

They sat on the sofa to drink the tea. The boy could not look at the man and the music just went round and round, petty and persistent and smiley.

The man made fish fingers for tea.

'Would you like a bath? Or anything?'

The boy woke up from a dream that was a soup of his mother and a boy with a bleeding eye, and, from his memory of seeing her on the telly, the woman he loved best – physically confusing to him now the effect of the slits in her dress showing the white skin – and a nightmarish bike he could not pedal. It faded abruptly, a residue left, a weight carrying him back into sleep.

When he woke again the man was standing over him, his shorts pulled down and his strengthless baby-fat stomach hanging over his hand as it flapped at his cock, his humiliating balls rucked up in a red and green waistband.

The boy lay mortified and still, finally void of his own will, and the man snuffled as if he were crying. The man's eyes were squeezed shut behind his little glasses and as he tipped his head to God a little light caught the lenses and made his look glazed.

And the fatty white thighs came forward into the edge of the mattress and the stomach jiggled and there was a bereft and glorious groan and the man's seed fell onto the boy's face and across where he lay and there was a stench of protein. And then the man fell to crying, to weeping, and the boy lay there sullied, and he was sure he heard harp music.

*Note: Picks up MSS again here*

The bungalow of the hermit was protected by some spell, for we lose sight of our hero and thus what happened that night is unclear. But such was it that the following morning we find our hero in reflective mood, rare for a character of such usual vitality.

That night it had snowed. [The record here is ambiguous and there is an implication this might be allegorical; it could be that it was simply a hard frost.] There was a duck, killed in the snow, and its head picked and spots of blood red in the snow. And our hero watched, and a jackdaw came down onto the carcass. It picked at the bird's flesh, its head jerking into the meat and into the snow and when it arose it flew to the bungalow's roof, a white cap of snow still upon its head and its legs like wooden sticks.

Peredur stood and compared the blackness of the jackdaw and the whiteness of the snow and the redness of the blood to the hair of the woman he loved best, which was as black as jet, and her skin to the whiteness of the snow, and the redness of the blood in the white snow to the two red spots in the cheeks of the woman he loved best. And he thought of his mother who was in the black place of death, and of the red speedball in the gym, and of the starched white tunics of the carers and nurses and of many other things.

And meanwhile, growing louder and louder, Arthur's voice. And he bade it come to him, to come and find him at that place. And there was then a great conflict in his mind, with his thoughts of his mother, and of that mixing and toiling with images of the woman he loved best, and his fantasy of greatness all clashing with the messages that Arthur sent, and sentences and images fell into a great toil, and so it was as if the real world were very distant to him at that moment. [Indeed, the text suggests an internal

We were like: Isn't that that kid?

We looked at him standing there, in the snow.

The one what smashed that guy's eye. Years ago.

It was like he was in a trance.

Kay went up to talk to him and stopped his bike right in front of him but he didn't move or nothing. Just stood there, staring like. Down at this gross bird what we couldn't see 'til we found it there later.

So Kay being Kay gets the hump and starts calling him a twat and lifting up his bike like in a wheelie, 'cept he wasn't moving. Just drawing attention. Then he went to riding round and round the kid, trying to get a rise out of him, 'Hey, Ape Frog, Ape Frog!' slushing and spraying up the snow with his wheels. It was that crap snow, not enough and it was already sloppy, wouldn't hold together. We couldn't throw snowballs from it. And he just stood there, swear blind, Priestland's pass now, staring down at that duck or whatever it was, holding this old curtain pole or something he'd picked up, like it was some great staff. Kind of obvious it was going to kick off, looking back. Bearing in mind how he was last time we'd seen him. But Kay's kind of stupid like that. He was calling the kid all sorts by then and riding closer and closer.

Well, no shock, but he finally got the kid's goat. Smashed him right off the bike he did. Right under the jaw. Well, we were running straight off.

*The pole hit Kay under the jaw with a sickening crunch. He came off the bike over the saddle and hit the ground with a snap and for a few metres the bike kept going, wheeling and listing until it careened wildly into the ground.*

We thought he was dead. Didn't move once he hit the ground and we heard the snap of his arm going from miles off. And that kid just stood there holding the pole. Like he was deep in thought.

Well, we reckoned Kay needed an ambulance. We reckoned best thing was to get on the right side of the kid. Like, what with various scraps coming up and them all getting a bit more heavy with us being older. He could be handy. And Kay was giving it the 'you fucking go and talk to him' and all that, but then he had taken the piss a bit.

So I went up to the kid, quiet like, trying to make it proper clear I didn't want any trouble.

'He shouldn't have bothered you, man,' I said. 'You were obviously thinking something through.'

The kid stood there for a while not looking at me. You have to understand. Being around him there was this kind of weird electricity.

'He was taking the piss,' he said.

Then I saw the ripped-up duck down there at his feet.

'He's that tall one, isn't he?'

I was looking down at the duck.

'Always throwing his weight around.'

I looked up from the duck, the little drops of blood about it.

'His arm's broke,' I said.

'Tell me,' he said. 'Is he really one of Arthur's sort?'

I didn't know what the fuck he meant. There was

this vague bell going off that he'd said that before, couple of years ago when he was all dressed up like a looney tune.

'He is,' I told him. Seemed the best plan.

Then he had this weird little smile to himself. Swear blind, he looked as mad as Andy Powell.

'I've been looking for you,' he said. 'I'm ready now.'

Then he gave me this big hug. That kind of stumped me.

The boy stood in Gwalchmai's room and Gwalchmai said 'Here, borrow some of mine.' And he set about digging out a shirt and other things for Peredur to wear. 'Better get a shower first,' he said.

When he came from the shower he sprayed himself generously with deodorant and gelled his hair and when he was dressed both boys looked pretty much the same. Then they went out to meet the others.

The entrance to the club was roped off and squat mushroomy bollards held the plush rope. A fog had fallen.

They had drunk on the bus and were laughing deliberately and went ahead of him into the club.

Peredur hesitated, watching them disappear through the door. He was afraid he would not be let in, but with the drink and the fog that had come after the snow he felt odd and like in some sort of spell.

When he stepped up to the door he heard the most incredible music. The music was physical. And moved by that, he stepped inside.

The instant he did so, the world changed. He found himself, not in some grey building on a worn street, but in a magnificent glittering place. It was crammed with people so good looking it took his breath away. They were dancing, joining hands, their movement captivating in the shattering light, white trainers flashing in the neon strobes, separate animals somersaulting from the ground.

The colour of their clothes was spectacular. The boys wore caps, and the lights caught in the girls' hair. He felt the watery edges of drink. It was captivating.

Gwalchmai came to him and said, 'Take this'. There was a smiling face on the pill. 'World's your oyster,' he said. He grinned and spoke through the music. He gave him two alcopops, a yellow and a red one. 'No water. Only rule!' Then he folded into the crowd. Peredur put the pill on his tongue.

White girl dimming in the blue light. The pump. The thump. The feeling going through you. The bodies move as one, but the isolated faces stand out, minds dancing in their own places.

The music like a cushion, like a place for your head, your bare arms, small skirt for the easily led; man-made lightnings in the man-made night, graced with looseness though the space is tight.

The bass. The pace. The feel of being lifted. Your mind going away from it; being shifted. You let yourself forget things, want things buried by sound. Your worry's being buried, body's leaving the ground.

In the chill-out room scenes of small capitulations, bodies giving in to intentions intended for ages: collisions of people while the music rages, who'll regain distance in the morning, resume normal relations.

Re-vamped 70s' tracks, seething mass on the dance floor. Moving it. Watching it. And you're dancing and your dancing and you're letting in the music. You use it. And suddenly you know you won't need anybody ever, as long as you can sail into the music with a million pale people moving to the same force, like all the spray on one wave all riding the same white horse.

And you look at the fountains, the silver drinking fountains. The water continuously from them, a silver thread. And when you go to one you see the myriad lights fall spinning in the water, a thousand coloured fish. The water pouring forth and the drops of condensation forming on the silver of the dish.

And you see yourself there mirrored, and you stare mesmerised, the smooth deliberate moving of the water so different from the dancing, bodies relaxing, tensing, grooving, so chosen – water drop choosing amidst all this trying to lose choice. Choosing falling.

The pump. The thump. An anonymous glance. Then you're taking in water and you're back in the dance.

'I don't know if I blame myself.'

You can see how she might have been then, a younger body. They can be feral and heartbreaking and pretty, girls like her, but they don't last. She still wears all the gold on her hands.

'I couldn't imagine it.'

I can see that his mother would have been like her.

'He was different. Different odd.'

'He get fixated on you?'

She nods.

'We were kids,' she says.

She moves the baby to the other knee so that she can organise a cigarette. Already she has the pinched mouth women can get from that. There's an open packet of biscuits on the table and she offers me one.

When they pulled him from the club there was a thin morning light. The last fawn slush of snow had gone. He had lost all sense of time.

They were in the gradual morning light. There was a strange displacement to them there. They looked incongruous in their lurid clothes. Their sweat chilled, the spell passed.

Peredur looked at Angharad, a white girl dimming in the blue light. They waited for the bus.

He watched her hands on the pale burger. Behind her the golden arches of the **M** sat like they gave her angels' wings.

He looked at all the rings on her hands, the bangles and the charm bracelet all hung with toys – a golden lock, a golden heart, her golden initial, A, like she had hands full of gold. It hit him in his stomach to be around her.

When he asked her out she said no: 'I don't want you.' He had mistaken the sick feeling for love. He told her so. The others were over smoking by the bins.

'Well I don't love you,' she said, 'and I will never want you, ever.'

She'll change her mind, he thought. I'll make her change her mind. First loves and some loves after that are about conviction, not feeling.

He stood there before her, reddening, and she felt sorry for him but was not interested. He stared at the charms – a key, a golden pussy cat that looked some-how like a lion. And she told him again, 'I don't want you. Stop being weird,' but there was a fossilising happening.

Peredur stared at her. To her he looked caught out and abashed but there was a violence rising in him. I'll make you, he said. He built up a great speech within himself. I'll make you then. I'll go out from here, and one day you'll know about me, and you'll wish you said yes. You'll beg to be with me.

When he left he carried with him the death of his mother and those bones he had made broken. He had with him the stain of the harpist, which he couldn't wash off, the stink of the corridors in the secure home. He had the smell of singed hair and piss and the sight of a tattered dress; he had the humili-ating pictures of himself on his bike. The arm bands and pads, and a vision of an eye busting at its root, the immediate seashore sound of that boy's breath. I'll show you, he said. Fuck this. Fuck this world. And all of this he said within himself. And he took all of this with him. And it was on his back like a stone.

# BIRD, BLOOD, SNOW

*Incident Number:* XXXX

It would appear he came over the ridge on the high road and dropped down into the above detailed area of town.

Damage was done to the pub sign. He then entered the Golden Lion. Present was the landlord, (----, 6'2", 61yrs) and two regulars who were playing darts at the time, (----, brown hair, 5'8", 22yrs, ----, blond, 5'2", 24yrs).

According to his account the said landlord challenged the youth regarding the sign he had damaged. The youth ignored the landlord and 'walked through to the family bar' which was at the time empty of customers.

At that point the landlord's wife (----, 5'2", 58yrs,19 stone) and daughter (----, 30yrs, 5'10") came into the family room from the kitchen to lay up the tables.

According to the account, the landlord and the two regulars followed the youth into the room and that is when the trouble started.

The daughter states that she asked the youth to leave and admits to threatening that the locals would soon be in and that he would be forcibly ejected if he did not leave of his own accord. (Note: it is unlikely the youth was aware of the volatile reputation of the area.)

This made him violent. It is unclear why, but the youth then assaulted Mr ----, one of the regulars. In attempting to intervene, the other regular Mr ---, was also grievously hurt.

The daughter states that she continually advised her father to call the police, but he admits to holding off, admitting that at the time he 'preferred to deal with the issue himself'. He admits this was a mistake.

Before leaving, the youth was heard to be 'shouting and raving'. It is unsure what he was raving about.

They came across a bike saddle, torn off, the padding weathered and tattered, and when they had ridden around part of the mountain, they discovered in a stream, lying twisted and half-broken and rusted, the rest of the bike.

As they were looking at the bike, they heard a whistle like that of a shepherd tending his flock, and suddenly, on their left, they saw a good number of sheep. Behind the sheep, at the top of the mountain, the shepherd appeared.

They called to him and asked him to come down. He shouted in response, asking what brought them to this place. Even from where they were they could see he was elderly. They asked him to come down.

'Found that bike, have you? On Hook it's been there six months. Tell me: have you come across the owner?'

'We haven't seen anyone. Found the saddle though. Not far from here.'

'I saw it. Left it where it was myself. Don't want nobody accusing me of anything. Nothing to do with me.'

'You know whose bike this is?'

'I know I saw some kid, some time ago, over the edge fields. He was riding it then pushing it, riding it then pushing it. That very bike there. He looked touched if you ask me. Wasn't right. He stood out bizarre in the posh tracksuit he had on. Had half a mind to talk with him, but he stayed off.'

'Any ideas where he went?'

The old man nodded out to the deepening hills: 'Out there somewhere. He went off. Getting on and off the bike, trying to ride it. Getting off it, getting back on it.

'Didn't think of him again really until a few days later when he crossed paths with one of the other shepherds. Just went up to him and started to punch and kick him, then went up to the quad bike and took his flask and a pasty and bag of crisps and ran off.

'We went and looked for him then for almost two

days. Out there,' he nodded to the hills. 'We found him in the hollow of a huge oak. He came out as gentle as you please. His clothes were torn and his face so changed I hardly recognised him. But you couldn't mistake those clothes. I was shocked how young he was, seeing him up close.

'We told him to just come and ask when he needed food, not take it by force. We thought we'd got through to him. He was on the verge of tears. Said he was sorry about the stuff before, taking the food. He wouldn't tell us who he was.

'And then, halfway through saying something, he stopped and went quiet. We didn't say anything, waiting to see what would happen, feeling sorry to see him like that, like some kind of craziness had come over him. Then in a great fury he jumped up and attacked the man closest to him, with so much violence and so much anger that if we hadn't dragged him off he would have beaten and bitten him to death. He was screaming, mad things. Still screaming when he ran off. It was impossible to follow him.'

– Well, that's our man.

– Our boy, said the other policeman.

They sat for a while on the quad bikes they had used, looking out at the central scale of those hills.

– He doesn't justify a helicopter.

– It's been a while, said the younger one. The comment was tacit and gently loaded. The tough weather was coming in.

– I vote we just see if he turns up, said the other

Seeing the bike in the stream there... you see, all you hear is how violent I was, but there were things leading up to that. Things that weren't told. That would not be part of the myth.

One of the other kids came running and said they'd put my bike in the stream. It was the most precious thing I had and I'd been searching for it.

There was a little stream at the edge of the estate and along it for a part a low brick wall about chest high to me back then.

They'd taken my bike and put it over the wall. It wasn't actually in the stream but it was scratched and one of the stabilisers was bent where they had dropped it over. The plastic saddle box was torn off and in the stream. It had been carried down but was caught in some weed that floated there, looking like it would get free anytime and be gone.

I had to get into the stream to get the saddle box out. It was cracked. The striped stickers that were stuck to it were peeling off and ruined. The hinges of the lid were permanently broken.

I tried to get the bike back over the wall. I struggled and got it over. The tyres were let down, and the saddle twisted round on itself. I didn't understand.

– And what did you do?

It was two of the older kids. Three or four years older than I was. They were in their front gardens when I wheeled the bike past them and they laughed and mocked. I was crying. I was distraught.

I took the bike home then went back to them. One of them had gone in but the other was still in his garden. I genuinely don't remember what he was doing.

The garden hose was lying there like a snake and I picked it up and swung it at him. He did not see it coming. The water gurgled and flew with each whip and I beat him until he cowered and bled.

After a while he managed to get inside.

— Do you think this is why your mother took you
   away?

It was.

— You remember the estates though?

I remember the estates. I didn't understand. I really
didn't understand. Because of the fear my father had
caused, the children of those he frightened took it
out on me. He was dead by then.

A time before that they tied me to the climbing
frame. There was a climbing frame there for us to
play on, the grass all worn away in dry patches
around it, and they tied me to the frame with my
own shoelaces.

I used to be something of a plaything for the girls
there, when I was so tiny, and I think it made the
boys jealous.

They said they were going off to get nails, and that

they would crucify me like Jesus.

They made me drink puddle water out of my shoe. They said it was poisonous. They said it would mean I would stay alive when the nails went in. So I would feel them. I'm not supposed to remember these things. I was very little. I was too little to do anything.

(At this he paused for quite some time.)

I wouldn't always be little, though.

    – Did you get the other one? The one who'd put your bike in the stream.

Not then. I got someone who laughed about it though.

I threw a large stone into his back and he crunched up like a spider dropped in water.

His father got hold of me. He bit me. That was the strangest thing.

Life – the way it runs for us – is so determined by gatherings of little accidents. Stones that change the course of the stream.

This was his attempt to return to innocence. To repeat the action of his mother, in removing himself from forces that would do harm to him. That would demand a violent response.

So he went 'into the wilderness'. But what did he find? A quad bike. The same machine that startled him so much when he was an infant: a thorough reminder of the poor deer. Again, the trigger: and violence was the result.

The same, an accident – a misheard word. Arthur's Court. What are the chances? But what is life but reaction to chances?

> – But why violence? When he was trying to get away from it. When it sickened him. He was aware. He had a voice telling him...

...and some other voice coming like a sharp whisper out of way back in his breed: 'sic 'im, boy, sic 'im.'

You can't shirk your genes.

The wind swung and the rain came in from the North and that had changed things.

He knelt in the wet ground over the sheep and tried to tear off the fleece. He tore so hard the quick of his nails hurt, but it would not come up.

The head was unusually floppy from the broken neck and a bone in the foreleg shin was out through the skin. A precise line of blood had come from its mouth with the fall and it had gone into a red lacquer.

He looked at the sheep. The eyeball seemed unnaturally big and still frightened.

It was a scraggy mountain sheep and he had found it wandered away from the flock. Its fleece was away in places but the obvious red squiggle of marker dye was there, and a dry bramble was caught up in the wool like a ring.

He had driven the sheep over the small quarry that the stone for the ruined walls about the place was from and when he got down to the sheep it was passive and dead.

He had not been in the wilderness long but he had lost weight quickly and his strength had stubbornised into a leverage. He was surprised at the weight of the sheep and tried to butcher it there.

He beat repeatedly with the sharp stick at a bald place of the sheep's neck but the hide resisted and then he pushed and leaned on the stick but still it would not go through. Then he looked down at the splintered bone of the foreleg and tore this out and with that sharp edge finally got through the skin.

He had no idea of butchery and he ripped and tore now at the meat of the sheep. He had seen a deer in that leap, and he wanted to dehumanise it.

He scraped and pulled at the sheep until he had recovered a shapeless pile of meat and was exhausted by the physical geography of the animal. It confused him that it had not bled very much. His nails hurt.

When he ate the first lump, he was sick.

We didn't recognise him at first. Looked like one of them junkies that come in now and then, all starey and away off the planet somewhere. Had this kind of crazy look. He was filthy. Bones of him all sticking out. Big bulgy eyes. A torn dirty sheepskin over his back that made his shoulders look bulgy. Skinny and bulgy.

Kay was out, as usual, straight over there. Swear down we didn't know it was him then, but it makes it a bit ironic.

'Where you from, squire? Where you from?' Kay. Always the same. And talk about history repeating itself, he didn't say nothing. So this time Kay just charges the guy with a shopping trolley, not knowing who it was. Thump. Right into his leg. He's a twat, sometimes, Kay.

We picked the guy up, still not clicking who he was like. It was like he was properly stoned. Didn't say anything. Like he's in shock or something. All skinny and bulgy. That should have given it away.

But there was a vulnerability there. I don't think we ever saw that before or again. That's maybe why we didn't click.

So Gwen gets all maternal instinct over him and we're making jokes about her catching stuff off him if she touches him, but actually I'm giving Kay grief again for being such a dick.

Anyway, there we were. It was later that day the other gang came.

Gwen and the rest of the girls and most of the younger kids move back, because it's sure this is going to be heavy. It's been coming for a while. And Kay's there, and me and Owain and everyone and the other gang lines up on their bikes. There were more of them than us.

I was feeling pretty sick if I admit it. It had got heavy. We weren't kids now. It was full on and out of hand but that was that. We weren't grown ups either.

And then Peredur stood up.

When everyone saw him get up and go and fight, they went behind the broken brick walls and on the roof of the old carriages and the burnt-out cars.

He had picked up an old iron bracing strap, holding it there like a sword. He seemed to signal. Come on then. And one of the other gang charged at him.

He struck the first in the visor so hard that his blade went into his teeth.

He stood motionless, the bike coming, the hiss and rasp of its speed building, then he hit him, lifting him out of his saddle. And he caught up the bike, and began to beat it down on the fallen guy. It all kicked off then.

And we knew, as soon as we saw him fight. Bulgy and skinny. The Ape Frog was back.

He was David to Goliaths. He was sling and stone both. He beat the boy until he bled from his mouth and ears, and he was sound and fury.

The people watched from about the high places and they looked down on him and called themselves his people then; and they saw him bear down with passion and wrath, violent and angry, eager and proud.

The blood dripped from his hand to his elbow and he cut down one after another. He reaped them.

He went back and forth against any who stood against him, so that they were filled with wonder at him; his sword was caked and dripping with blood and brains and the earth was heaped with the broken.

His fury rose as he gave such a sword stroke that the blade went through helmet and skin and bent the bars of the bike that came at him. And the ground then was pink with the blood and snow. And he was a wind upon the earth.

And then, above, a flock of geese. And he was a majesty amongst the ruin he had made, and the sky filled with their call; and he watched, and spread out his arms so the blood fell from him; and the sky was riot.

'You want to hear it? You really want to know? This is it, in slow motion.

'Gets to boiling. That's how it feels. Blood. Like it gets heated up. I feel my veins then, all hardening.

'Once it starts, that's when it all slows down. For me. I feel light and gliding, a bird distantly above.

'You can feel how far something has given in your fibres. Whether a bone's gone. Cheeks are the best. Like paper. Jaws. The pop of a jam-jar lid. There's a wildness gets in their eyes if you bust one of those.

'Noses we all know. Nose bone can break like old bark if you hit it upwards, feel it disappear up inside the head somewhere. Makes them quiet. A kind of mongy nghhing noise if they make anything. Hit them right and the eyes can blacken up pretty much immediately, like busted TV screens.

'Then there's the other bones of course. You can get a person all slopey with a collar bone, easy with something heavy. Not highly technical. Good, satisfying crunch when they go. Ribs are tricky. Sometimes they go, sometimes they don't. You kind of know when you've popped a lung though; easily confused mind with a cracked sternum: either way fuckers can't breath.

'Legs. Arms. Simple stuff. All angles really. Only so much weight they'll take. Fingers. Now. Fingers are fun. Panics people so you have to have control for that. Over them, I mean.

'That's breaking. Then there's bruising and tearing. Ears tear. You ever seen that?

'Don't look at me like that. You asked.

'It hurts you, you know, when you punch some-body's teeth. Teeth can go right into you.'

He went on to tell me how it feels afterwards. Brings a peace across him. A descended calm. Like snow.

Police Force: ...............
Division: .....................
Misc. Prop. No. ..............
Description of item: **Mobile phone.**
Identifying mark: ..............

---

LAB. REF.

CLIP ONE: You see the dogs. In the background there are the noises of the bikes. There's no time stamp. The light suggests it's dawn. The phone camera doesn't deal with the light well and there's often a bluishness to what we can see. A lot is unclear.

The shot swings away from the lurchers. It's unsteady now as the cameraman is walking. There's a group of kids. I'd guess fifteen, sixteen. No older than that. Their hands and faces look quartzy white, stand out.

You can hear the dogs, their sounds, the cameraman talking to them. CLIP STOPS.

NEXT CLIP: Close-up of an air rifle. (*Police detail* – Looks like Webley Raider 10, pneumatic, .22, likely modified.)

The dogs are whining and you can hear the kids talking. Frequent disruption of detail as screen glares and darkens. Phone dropped and everybody laughs. Picked up. Screen covered. A sleeve? (As phone is wiped.) In the time it's picked up see the bike spokes, a trainer. CLIP CUTS OFF.

NEXT CLIP: The kids move off on the bikes, the dogs on leads out in front them. You can clearly see Peredur. (Proof he was socialising with the gang at this time.) One of the kids is carrying another 'weapon'. (Crossbow? Inconclusive.) Jerky shot as the cameraman must mount the bike and start off. Sound of this bike drowns out anything from the rest of the group. Gathers pace. The clip continues until it CUTS OFF.

They headed out to the scrub forest, each with some deep private examination, though they were a group.

When they got to the edge of the forest some of the boys went on foot into the overgrowth with the tracking dogs and the others came behind in two groups along the dirt paths either side of the scrub so there were two flanks holding the chase dogs straining and lurching on leads in front of them. In that light, the brindle of the chase dogs looked mineral.

They went through the sallow soft on their pedals, following the dogs. They could hear the cracking and the pushing of the boys in the overgrowth.

When the yelp came, it was hard and percussive.

They slipped the chase dogs and they bounded away and flashed out into the sallow and they heard the sound of a bigger animal and the whip of branches crashing off in front. And they shone their lights and sped shouting in their flanks along the two paths.

The deer bolted. It had stayed still as long as it could, the stink of the incoming dogs thickening like a wave in the air. And there was a tipping, when the deer knew, and it ran.

The sallow wood was netted with cycle paths, fudgy and slick with mulched leaves and a high panelled fence of wire demarked the far side of the area, cutting it off from new building land. It was into this they drove the deer.

It sped ahead of the grey lurchers and burst from the cover and seeing the two flanks coming so bright with light it launched itself at the mesh and the dogs hit it. They were off their bikes and running now, and the others came out of the forest.

They regather the dogs and the deer bolts against the wire again and gives out a low guttural scream. Time seems to decelerate, the force of the deer's leap hanging it there for a while, the torchlight glittering electricity in the disturbed wire. There is a thwack, an air-gun pellet spreading its force and flattening on the animal's hide, delaying there by its all-forward force before its power is gone through as pressure into the receiving muscle, a sound energy seemingly, travels into the bone. And the deer drops.

CLIP: The deer drops from the fence. The thud (of a crossbow bolt?) They fall to kicking it.

*Something snapped. And I understood with this sickening, brutal act I needed help.*

He came to us of his own accord. This is positive. It suggests he is aware, at least periodically, of his delusion.

Given the repeatedly violent outcomes of his delusional episodes it's possible he is at odds with the delusion itself; that he can't *quite* believe it, precipitating a combat; which itself suggests there is a personality there we can 'get back to', that actually wants to exist.

Dropping the medical speak for a moment, I think locking him away would make him more violent, and more insane.

– So your suggestion?

We recommend he is committed to a psychiatric facility, for his safety, and for the safety of everybody else. He will be less threatened there.

   – Can he be cured?

Some mental illnesses are just that. People get ill for a while, they recover, they get over it – like a common cold. I'm not sure this boy's condition is so simple. There are too many factors. It's more like an inherited disease.

Worst-case scenario, if he can't adjust – or we can't adjust *him* – we can actually make him a world that will sustain his delusion, and give him no cause to get violent. Main danger of that is, given the artificial stability, he could go on to try and control everybody outside that framework. It can give a fake sense of power and importance. But with the chronic, it's sometimes better than trying to medicate the thing out of existence. You invariably lose a lot of the positive parts of an individual's identity when you do that.

– He has been hellish violent. There's EST, of
   course. If he doesn't change.

Remember *he* came to us. That was a cry for help.

From some viewpoint far away in his delusion he's
seen signs of a safe place, and he's approached that
safe place. He's shown acknowledgement. There's a
distance to go, but that's a large part of the battle.

– What made him?

A trigger, usually. Something referring back to his
childhood, a time he was happier.

# Might Be Of Help

Note - was (wrt Y Brenin
ie/ne was 'one of them'

**TAKEN FROM ESTATE** — v. young

Father dead,
brothers etc.

⚹ bullied
(bike incident etc.)

This really affected
him; becomes
later 'trigger'

**TO HOLIDAY VILLAGE**

Sees the deer being
chased + killed

removed from other
kids

(KEY MOMENT)

Mother becomes
Alcoholic, dysfunctional

Note Suggestion of
genetic disposition
to 'dependence' +
'mental weakness'?

**BOYS ON BIKES**

Note - to check -
think this Gwalch,
Owain + 1 other

**HE GOES OFF**
+ follows them

✳ **FIGHTS**

⚹
∘ **GIRL IN WENDY HOUSE**
-"accident" of Princess/Knights
- gave him an false 'idea' of
how to behave
around others

Stick in boy's eye          (Police)

age 7/8 yrs          etc. x 16
**BOXING**

"uncle"
Point of stability

**FOSTERED x 2** — doll boy

He "destroys" this
stability because of
fear of having it
taken away from him

**RUN OFF ‡ 1**

becomes ill

what was
illness ?

**KIND WOMAN** (in dress)

∘ **VAGUE - need more work on this**

**CHILDREN'S HOME**

(11/12 yrs?)

— attacks nurse

**RUNS OFF ‡ 2**          "HARPIST" ✳

⊛ As far as I
know doctor's
unaware of this.
v. reluctant to
tell it. Was there
more than he
admits to ?

**GANG**

lives with
Gwalchmai?

Clubbing

Pub sign
vandalised

rejection          Angharad

⚹ 1st use of drugs -
( psychotic episode )

∘ Note - can be
trigger of latent
mental problems
(e.g. schizophrenia)

attacks shepherd

**RUNS OFF ‡ 3**

(is vague on
this          stays out? time?
How long?

**BACK TO GANG** (15/16 yrs old)
∘ **BIG FIGHT**

**DEER HUNT** — accepted
properly by gang

i.e./ the trigger -
too much for him. Seeks
help - OR having been accepted
= structure, breaks structure again — **HOSPITAL** — 16 yrs old

# BIRD, BLOOD, SNOW

*[The following draft from notes and tape recorded-material. Originals taken.]*

I'm just watching the three of them, playing some board game. Clackety. Clackety. They're infantile. With their shaved heads, their pyjamas. They don't even get the game and it's too confusing for them and after every baby-rattle shake of the dice they argue. I think they just like the sound of the clackety plastic cup. They laugh like truly ill people. It angers me that I find it hypnotic myself, that clackety plastic cup. Part of me wants to rescue them. To put them from this misery.

I get up and I go over to the three nurses and it's like my body doesn't come with me. Like it stays there watching the infantile men with their shaved heads and pyjamas. Feels sometimes, my body, that it's too heavy for my mind to pick up – heavy like wet clothes – so I just leave it sometimes now. Let my mind free of the weight. It sits there, in those same angular pyjamas, that crinkle and rub and I don't know why, why they dress us ~~in these borrowed~~

~~robes~~ like this.

And one of those nurses looks at me. She's looking through my mind right next to her over to the slow body I've left still sitting, but she doesn't know that I feel a proximity. That I imagine I hear her.

'Such a shame to see a handsome boy like you so beaten.' Oh! How she spoke of my glories.

And I say to her, up there right close, 'no one has beaten me,' to reassure her; and I say it whispered straight into her mind, 'no one *will* beat me.' I implant it; push the words I say right into her corners. ~~I wallow in her fissures. And as I do that, I can feel her terror at the world~~.

I look out through her eyes, see my body sit. My dummy self. My decoy.

Whatever they have given me has split my body from my mind. Has weighted me physically.

'Don't worry about me,' I say. Whisper it inside her. Clackety. Clackety. 'Don't worry about me.'

The buzzer sounds and through the glass screen I see the doctor coming in. He's black, a huge man. He wears a bizarre light on a headband, like one big eye.

There is a sudden absence of clackety, the infants clear the game away. ~~It has a specialness, I believe, that glass. It magnifies him, and he is not the great size he seems to us, out here, this side, in the day room~~.

The nurses go in to the doctor, into the glass station where they often sit like spiders in the centre of their web. (And I cannot penetrate, I cannot penetrate his glass, cannot follow them in, retreat, my mind, into my heavy body.)

They take his coat to hang up on the door. ~~It magnifies only him, the huge doctor~~. He sits down. And when he has collected his thoughts and rested, he looks up at me and asks who I am.

His glass cannot stop me hearing her. I inhabit her chemicals now. I imagine my mind walks a thin wire to her: 'Lord,' said the maiden, 'the fairest and noblest young man you have ever seen.' (She means me.) 'And for Warburton's sake, and your own pride; be patient with him.'

For I am a new thing to him.

*Transcript from psychiatric interview:*

- So, who are you?
- You have my notes.
- I have notes on you, but I'm interested in who you feel you are.
- Who are you?
- It's unimportant. I'm here to help you. The important thing is for us both to work out who you are, and how we can work on you feeling better.
- Where are you from?
- It's not important...
- Who you are and where you're from and why you're here. All these things will determine what you decide I am.
- I'm really not here to discuss...
- What's that eye for?
- I don't think...
- I've seen them do that. A big headlight mounted on a truck cabin. The rabbits go blind, or mesmerised. Makes them easier to shoot. Is that

why you have one eye like that? To blind me
too?

– It says here you came to us of your own accord.
That you sought medical help. [*There is a pause.*]
Who is Arthur?

– Why don't you turn your light on?

*From the _____ MSS. Referencing the* Serpent and the Stone *fairy tale*

For that night previous, our hero, in his bedrugged state [i.e. psychiatric medication] fell to dream. He dreamt of a one-eyed man, a man that was black of skin; and it was as if the dream was some narration:

He dreamed of a big man and the coal was engrimed into his skin. It was as if he had internalised the coal. His hair and skin were black. He had one eye.

The man was a big man and he worked within the mountain.

*Many years ago, a great serpent of timber had been trapped under the mountain, and – forced to live there, starved of light and air – turned black.*

*For centuries it wandered underground the hill, growing until it stuck and died amongst the passages and wends.*

*All men are part of a long line. And the one-eyed man still had the thread of his line in him.*

*His father's fathers had been woodcutters and they had taken timber from the wooden serpent when he lay upon the* land. And so the one-eyed man — though he was not then one-eyed, for this was to come — followed the serpent into the ground to continue that work.

They built up a great cairn and from it a tunnel down to where the serpent lay. And many men went; and they cut the stone from the serpent's tail and sent it above ground, and the man who held that stone in his hand had as much gold as he wished in his other hand.

And this is how he lost his eye: they worked with picks and spades to hack the monster's wall, and there in the dark, no bigger than a lizard's scale, a shard came from the wall into the big man's eye.

And it damaged his sight.

They have given me victuals. Black pills and white, red pills and grey.

In a while I start to feel my mind gather a heaviness, a fluid heaviness of water, like it's pouring itself back into my slow body, a hole dug in wet sand. Like everything's mingling.

He wants to kill me, this oppressive man. I'm feeling my travelling wire tighten with the weight of the rest of myself, hear it sing with tension. Since you have been an oppressor for so long, I shall make sure that you will not be so again.

He will not admit who he is. This coal miner. Even his black hair silvers like coal. That's in this vile white light.

He's telling me of my road ahead. He is a misbeliever; he denies I have a strength. He talks repeatedly of cutting downs, of suffering – of an hypnosis.

He tries to slow me. Sings out: you are not strong.

You are not strong enough. But I am a hole in wet sand. A hole dug in wet sand. And I will kill him if the wire snaps.

## Card # blot 04: Peredur Ap Efrog

The face of a fox terrier, a riffled coated dog, close up. An older dog, whitened at the beard. It's missing an eye (it's right eye), lost it in a fight with a rat, perhaps. Or another dog. It changes completely if you turn it.

Now it's a dragon, from above. It's wings out, part folded. Something a medieval knight might fight. Or have on his shield, perhaps.

- Something from the Middle Ages?

We're always in the middle ages of something, aren't we?

Card # blot 06: Peredur Ap Efrog

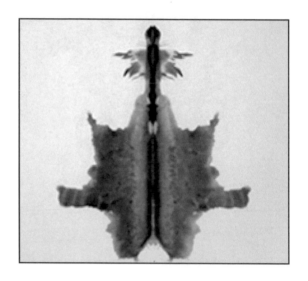

It's obviously a vagina. But turn it on its side...

Like this.

Trees, a lakeside bank, reflected in still water. It's evening. Late summer.

Card # blot 02: Peredur Ap Efrog

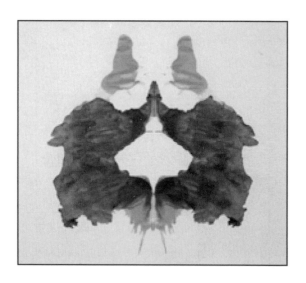

Witches. Spelling, touching hands. Their hooded garbs, loose sleeves, red hoods. Their thin pinky goose necks. But, turn it. On its side. See their fate. Each of them...

Kneeling and bleeding. Her own blood. Dying. Her reflection in a shining, polished floor.

[I could only make black and white copies; on the test there are blotches of red around the 'feet' (low, where the two shapes join as the card is upright), and the 'heads' are red and the 'necks' pinkish.]

# BIRD, BLOOD, SNOW

Police Force: ................
Division: ......................
Misc. Prop. No. ..............
Description of item: **Notebook** recovered
from S.O.C. Doctor's notes, handwritten.
Identifying mark: .............

---

LAB. REF.

Patient shows unusual awareness of his situation, and
highly (surprisingly) developed verbal skills. Able to
respond with sophisticated answers. (Remember he
grew up apart from other kids, developing his own
worlds and probably with plenty of early input from
his mother, before things went wrong. This 'betrayal'
of a seemingly utopian infant world would add to
adult dysfunction. Note also: takes a degree of imagination and creativity to build delusion as he has.)

He has vivid (visual) imagination. Approach to RTs
v. advanced. Note patient's awareness: stock answers,

then complex pictorial response suggesting capacity to build story.

Suggests he is [*'is' underlined*] in charge of violent side. Has a concept of serenity (see response to blot #6), but [*several words, handwriting illegible*].

Unsure whether to continue one-to-one sessions. Request ♂ chaperone next session. He is surely physically strong. His coordination is good. Recommend increase app. of mild sedative med.

– And if he doesn't?

– Co-operate with his initial treatment? We will be forced to take further steps. It's the last thing we want to do. There's inevitably side effects. Always are. The first step would be EST.

– Shock therapy.

– Yes.

– That has to be voluntary. Does it not?

– There's voluntary, and 'voluntary'.

# CYNAN JONES

From *Western Journal of Psychiatry*, Obituary

The medical and psychiatric community today pays respect to the memory of Doctor H. Brubaker

Doctor Brubaker was assaulted while working at the psychiatric unit of the ----- Institution. It was a violent and severe assault. Despite the concerted efforts of medical staff, he failed to recover from his injuries.

Our thoughts and feelings go out to his family and to the staff at the facility who are deeply shaken by the tragedy.

It is understood that the offending patient has been moved to a secure psychiatric facility.

# BIRD, BLOOD, SNOW

*Note to self:*

I do not want to 'create' him. Do not add things to him that are not there.

Be careful not to 'write' him. Be aware: I am a writer. The writer's job is to 'build' characters into whole beings. Do not fill in gaps with untruths just to do this. Resist inevitable pressure from editor to do this. Ask for more time.

Do not falsify a narrative line. Work harder to get the truth out.

The women got up and welcomed him. Their curves were diminished in the starched white clothes, and there was a measured, round softness to the way they talked. There was a trained, unthreatening thing to them. It created a tension, like a quiet room.

As they started to talk he could see a gurney approaching, and a prone man upon it.

One of the women met the gurney and helped the man from it to a bed; then Peredur watched as she bathed his head with a flannel, and applied some ointment to his temples and cleaned off a gluey stuff that was on him. And she talked that gentle way, and the man seemed to stare vacantly out. Then he made a bizarre guttural noise, as if some statement to Peredur, and it reminded him of the deer caught in the fence, that noise, and it went through him.

Two more prone bodies came into the ward on their gurneys, and the nurse went rhythmically about the same process, bathing and settling the men into their beds.

Then Peredur asked one of the patients who was with him, 'Why are they like that?'

'Oh! There's a monster in that room,' he said. He grinned cruelly, but left it at that.

They took him along the corridor, and behold, he came across the fairest woman he had ever seen, sitting behind a desk where they pulled him up and bade him to sit. In his mind he was going to fight the dragon. That is what he tried to believe.

'Will you be very good for me and swallow this,' she asks. And she gives him a small, smooth pill.

She is smooth voiced as she tells him, 'It's ok. I'll be here. Count backwards, for me,' she says. 'Count back. Ten, nine. Eight, seven...' Her whisper like a receding sea.

He is unconscious when they hit him with electricity and some deep place inside him starts at the spark, a vision of two dogs running through a forest, bags of picked-up shit at eye-level in the trees, and the glittering of light in the fence as a deer busts into the mesh.

They have wheeled him into the sun.

The lawn slopes away manicured to the river behind the fence. Again, high-wire panels. The ground roughens towards the water, sedge and iris. There is a fringe of willows.

He looks up at the home: the long facia of the day room. The orderlies and nurses going back and forth, answering the patients' calls.

Those inside, through the patio glass, look grey, dark; those outside – in their white clothes, their borrowed robes – bright.

When one goes in, they turn dark; when one comes out, they brighten white.

There is a laburnum on the riverbank, dying of some fungal disease. Half of it is yellow flowers, like it's half on fire, half dead.

Beyond the trees and beyond the river he sees a man walking with his dogs. Two greyhounds folding with speed in front of him.

Even from here he sees that they have been through wet ground, strangely three feet each darkened with dirt and a fourth clean, as if they have each lost a shoe.

He lifts a hand to the man who greets him back. He wells with tears, and the world blurs, as if the river has spilled out.

Re: Patient: P. Ap Erfog. (sic.)

To the Board,

He seems to be responding well. There is a marked improvement in his patience, and he is calmer. (Expected, with the EST, and the medication, but nevertheless an excellent platform for improvement. I hesitate to say rehabilitation as I suggest his condition is far too chronic.) He even socialises infrequently with the other patients.

He is surprisingly articulate. (Of course, he could not have built such complex delusions were he not, so I don't know why I say surprisingly.) He has acknowledged himself that his format has been to destroy any situation he begins to see the structure of. He accepts this is probably on account of being taken away at the wrong time from a place he felt connected to. He no doubt bundles this trauma with the loss of his father, (i.e. father figure, that vacuum replaced by his Arthur character.)

We have talked about overcoming this fear of 'place'. It causes some trouble with the other patients but he now has a favourite seat in the day room. This is a start. (He is actually claiming a 'location'.) He has also taken to collecting cups, which he is very possessive of. (Again, this causes some trouble, but does indicate that he is beginning to develop a sense of the ownership of things, and therefore of permanence to an extent. There is also the more abstract relevance of the cups to consider: the receptacle, a thing expectant to be filled, a 'female' object; an incredibly personal device – some would say a surrogate breast – that can deliver nourishment, water – in that sense, a maternal replacement – etc, etc.)

This improvement aside, I do not suggest we cease EST at this time. Intend to continue treatment as we have it.

The guy in the red pyjamas comes up to me. He has a sidling way to him. If nothing else, my instinct is intact, and I can tell when someone's wheedling.

'What do you want?' I say.

The conversation we have is interesting.

Turns out one of the nurses will use her hand for twenty quid. 'She'll clean her hand with her mouth for another tenner,' he says.

One guy says for a hundred she did it with her mouth from the start then spat it back into one of those little paper pill cups. He's kept it. There's still a faint trace of her lipstick on it, mad fuck. His eyes are bright.

He follows me through to the day room. We are to be 'Sociable' in here, it says. She's in there, sitting with some of the placid ones.

I have made myself dislikeable. The others visibly tense when I come amongst them now. I tell them to get away and sit down with the nurse when they leave. She asks me if there's anything I want. She's not stupid.

The red pyjamas man is gleaming at me, shifting from one foot to the other like he needs to piss with the excitement.

'Not me,' I say. 'Edlym.'

He's nearly as red as his pyjamas when she walks him off to his ward. Amazing what humiliations people will undergo for a little handout.

He couldn't do it for himself. He couldn't quite have the faith in himself to get away with wearing those red pyjamas confidently. He needed me.

I feel myself spinning. Thinking what she's doing for him I start thinking about that harp music again, the acid mess drying on my skin. Feel the spin. Like a mivvering of the mind.

You see, when I was a child I was hampered. I was taken away from things that I should have had the chance to work through. And thus, I guess, I built my own world of magic.

# BIRD, BLOOD, SNOW

I built my own world where I was king, where I ruled not only men and women and animals but clouds and stars and sky. I was invisible. I flew. I was a bird. No authority could keep me in or out. In my dream I built not only a world but remade myself as I would wish to be. I guess that's all.

Usually people make peace with the world and work out compromises so that the two will not hurt each other badly.

Well, some few do not make peace. And some of these are locked away as hopelessly insane and full of fantasy.

I know full well I choose now, one way or another, whether to climb aboard, let myself be spun up in my delusion; in the speed and whirl of it. Let the world off my merry-go-round turn into a blur. It's all choice. That's what the sane sometimes don't recognise. Most people live in a half-dream all their lives and call it reality. Just take a step. It's all just another tactic to get through. A tactic. A way of surviving. Kids know invisible friends aren't there but they prefer them to be.

The truth against the world? Huh! Get real.

And I see, my spinning eyes, the vortex of my mind suck up everything around me into its centre; I see the vegetable idiots here crash against furniture as I hurl them in their chairs, bones break through flaccid flesh as I break those down who are before me.

I can look up gloriously at the sky spilling in through my world's funnel, whatever light I want glimmering on the ripped bodies of the nurses here, their witches' robes shred, their hair out in clumps. I see it all, the edge of my whirl, and Arthur watching. If I want to. But I know it isn't real. Arthur. Arthur is a lucky coin in my pocket. A rabbit's foot.

That makes me insane. But change that name for God. For Jesus. They let people go to church here. They tell us faith will help us. But it's just having some conviction★.

[Note:] ★Conviction, sometimes, an artificially emphasised belief in something that allows you to take part in it, e.g. the laws of football. [Explore idea of him using delusion like a faith.]

# BIRD, BLOOD, SNOW

I go through to the ward. It's got late. I must have drifted off. I've been ESTd again. I can tell by the sticky that's still on my head; a tightness on my skin, like that spunk drying. It steals time from you. I feel as dry as hay.

It's oppressively hot and standard fans line the aisle, plugged in by the beds. The beds line the ward, most with curtains drawn. Just that thin nylon of privacy. It's the sounds that get you, though. The sounds are enough to drive you mad. It's not what you see but what you hear.

The plastic chairs have been arranged out in front of the ward television. A special treat. Like children, we are allowed up after a certain time, (they say it's vital we have a Routine); but they're letting us watch the concert tonight, in the ward. There was a vote. I'm sure there are those who don't want to hear it, but the world doesn't work that way. That's the problem with sound, smell, smoke. It reaches other people.

The large auburn-haired orderly is on the ward.

Already the television is on and you can see the tents of the festival and the pavilions and marquees and the glorious stage in the centre of it. And the pavilions and food vans with their canopies and the tents seem somehow to continue out into the ward with all the curtained beds here, like I could keep walking all the way onto that stage. I scratch away some of the dried gel from my head and watch it fall, a tiny snow. Again, I sense a little vortex, a delicious little vertigo.

I go to my bedside cabinet and collect my cups, my three precious cups – they help me feel Secure, Safe, I need them says the doctor, a reference point – and sit before the concert. It's as if I could step in, out of these distant tents, into that place. I try to shut out the noises of the other 'guests'.

And then, there she is. The camera rushes to her as she appears – a steady beat begins – frames her face, like she looks out at me from a window. But she seems close enough to touch. Beat. Beat.

Ah! That spin. Like a helicopter camera shot. And

I let myself roll in. I have never seen a more beautiful maiden. Arthur sits there smiling. She is dressed in gold. And I gaze at her. And she starts to sing.

I make my choice, choose to ignore the talking and muttering – why can't people be quiet? – and until the interval stay here, in this world of my own.

People are shifting about at the break in the concert. And some are staring at the half-time adverts and have finally shut up. I have a headache now, that post-shock headache.

I ask the orderly for something. 'Say,' I say. 'I'm feeling sort of edgy. Could you give me something? I need a little something.'

He's standing there by the waist-high cabinet with the electric fan whirling on top and the face of it scanning left to right, humming and throwing about the air in that area of the room.

He looks unconvinced. 'Just a little something,' I say, 'a leveller.'

I imagine being very small, riding into that wind-mill.

'Nurse told me to ask,' I say, and it's all I can do not to say 'the witch'.

He looks me up and down and takes his keys and opens up the cabinet and fiddles through it. I see into the treasure chest, jewels of pink and blue and foil, white pearls of pills, tablets and capsules of untold wealth.

He passes me two tiny pills and turns to get me water. I put them on my tongue.

So much of life is timing.

The nurse shouts and he hits me on the back, I cough the half-melted tablets out. He's not amused.

I watch the tablets slightly fizzing on the lino tiles, losing their shape at the edges, just a little like me.

When I can drop into my special place, everything is fine. As I've said, the real things blur. Then the damages I want on them can happen in my mind.

I think of the pills fizzing on the floor. My trouble comes with clarity. When I can't apply the brakes and go rushing into the face of reality. I should have had those pills. I'm accelerating. Feels like I'm tapping my broken brakes but the pads are worn, my mind spinning, a hot wheel carrying me straight head on at the wall of the world. Not good. But it's a choice as well. I've said that. Most of life is just steering into the skid. And they keep talking. They're talking while she's trying to sing.

That's what my mother did not understand: no

matter how you build them, the world will come crashing against your fences.

And that's it.

I dedicate this to her. They were talking through your music, maiden. And we cannot have that.

The first thing to go is the cabinet beneath the television which I rip out and hurl at the row of seats. They scatter. The television hits the ground with a plastic crunch.

I am instantly behind the cabinet, through the space it's made in the air, driving my fist into a face, its structure breaking and folding under my repeated force. Everyone is screaming now.

When he is so slick and bloody that my punches won't land properly I put him down and go after another.

It's a beautiful chaos now. Men flee before me. The curtains tear and beds go over. They come down like collapsed pavilions, like a broken camp.

I catch another by the foot and twist and twist until it hangs there like an apple in a bag. I don't see who it is, just hear the scream.

The ward throbs with the flashing orange light and is filled with the alarm, as if the room itself has reacted to the fear. I remember, years ago, the flock of geese passing over in their hundreds, hear the honk of the alarm.

I tip things and I smash things. You should see how many wires and cords are broken and stands pulled over, and how many curtain poles lie fallen on the floor.

I look up and Arthur is not smiling. 'It's a black day, a troubled day,' he says. 'It's a day, simply a day,' I say. 'You have a black and troubled mind, my Lord.'

I might have overdone it this time.

*The Incident with the Cups – from _____'s unfinished manuscript. [Some time after the incident above, after which medication and EST were stepped up. Perhaps the final 'violent act' before an even further increase in therapy, after which P. seems to have been fairly quiet for over a decade.]*

'Don't touch my cups. Don't touch my cups.' But they are determined to upset him.

They laugh manically, a high and insane un-right laugh, and the first parades with the yellow plastic cup, aping that he's drinking from it.

'My cup. *My* cup,' shouts Peredur. [It is likely that our hero was heavily medicated at this time and physically slow with it, and we can imagine the other patients knew it.]

'Fight me for it, fight me for it,' mocks the black-haired man.

Give the cup to me, the fair nurse says. And the black-haired man accedes. But then another. Mockery! This time with his china cup.

'My cup,' shouts Peredur. And again, this time, this other black-haired man hands the china to the nurse. And both times she lets Peredur have them, and he drank the blackcurrant squash, and passed his cup to a second nurse for safe keeping.

And then the ginger-headed giant, the big curly-haired slob, appeared, and danced there before Peredur with his glass tumbler, its pretty lines clutched there in his filthy podgy hands.

'My cups,' said Peredur quietly.

## CYNAN JONES

From *Coroner's Report; Incident No. XXXXX*

From the reports of witnesses it is clear the patient waited until the morning following the incident. This suggests significant planning and forethought correlant to the scale and nature of the injuries. They are not indicative of a spontaneous and uncontrolled attack.

First black-haired man: The neck is snapped. It is the clean break of a violent twist, rather than correlant with a fall or heavy blow. The fingers, numbering six, were probably broken after the act.

Second black-haired man: We removed two shards of a china cup from the eye sockets. They would have instantly blinded the victim, but were not deep enough to hurt the brain. Again the fingers are broken with clear determination. We were not sure what killed the man until we found the rest of the cup fed to him. It was likely he was then punched, the internal shards of china thus puncturing his insides.

Red-haired man: The hair is ripped out. Circular torsions on the face and skull correspond to the size of the base of a broken glass discovered near the scene. There are no fingers. It is likely he cut them off with the glass.

You see, there are lines. There are lines of humiliation you should not have to cross. I like my seat, and I like my cups. I told them not to touch my cups.

— And that was fourteen years ago.

The cups? Yes. That was fourteen years ago now.

— But you feel the need to talk about it, these last few months.

You asked.

— But you have not said yes before. To anyone.

# BIRD, BLOOD, SNOW

*A note found left upon his bed. Handwritten.*

I dreamed last night. I walked along a mountain, and on the other side I could see this place, this 'Fortress of Wonders', ha! Nestled here beside the river as it is. The soft, slow river. How peaceful for us.

And as I entered – the place, in the dream, was more of a hall inside – and the door opened, I saw the lame old guy who taught me to box. I saw Gwalchmai there beside him. Old friends. And I saw my little bike, all adorned. And Uncle patted that old bench and I saw the deer hunt embroidered, vivid there, not faded anymore, and I went to sit with them.

I was extraordinary then. I could have been put to good.

I used to be a rescuer of small things. My little goats.

*Beside the note were handfuls of pills. He had not taken his medication for weeks.*

And I saw then how it was. I will not be a deer in your wire. And I called for Arthur. And lo! He came.

*He had signed the note Ape Frog.*

# BIRD, BLOOD, SNOW

From *The Celtic Echo*

## Moment of Madness in Insane Asylum

Long-term inmate Peredur Ap Efrog (34), son of the infamous Carl Efrog, known as 'The Earl' in criminal circles, now deceased, was found guilty yesterday of what police have called 'a one man riot'.

'The unit is a secure unit for criminal patients with psychiatric problems,' said a spokesman, 'and they are set up to deal with dangerous behaviour, but this was extreme and pre-motivated. It took them by surprise.'

Ap Efrog had been an inmate of the facility for fourteen years and was undergoing therapy. 'He was also on medication, but seemingly somehow he managed to fool the staff, and he was not taking his tablets,' he said.

In an horrific attack, Ap Efrog killed several nurses. Staff from the facility have been asked not to talk to us, but we do know he believed them to be witches at the time. Final details of the casualties have not yet been released.

We can now reveal Ap Efrog to be the 'Child Terror' reported on many years ago by this very newspaper. Questions have to be asked why a child that dangerous – who terrorised local children for years – was allowed to grow up into such a dangerous adult.

A psychiatric expert, contacted by the *Echo*, said: 'He was not sane,' refusing to comment any further.

She's bleeding out now. They're coming for me. She's number three, but Arthur will go after the others.

Strange to watch them, through that unbreakable glass, trying to get to me. To hear the dull thump of them charging the door.

That filing cabinet won't move. I imagine all our little minds in it, scribbled down to little notes. All encased and kept in there.

She gurgles now. And as she does, her blood bubbles through the new mouth in her throat.

You failed witch. They cannot have me now.

They are trying now with chairs; it's funny, the strange vibrating noise of them bouncing off. The blue lights and the noise

# Peredur

## a synopsis

Peredur was the son of Earl Efrog who lived by fighting. He was too young to fight and his mother, a wise woman, fled with him to the wastelands. No one mentioned war or weapons to him, but every day he would go to the forest and throw holly darts.

One day he saw three knights but when he told his mother she fell in a dead faint. So he took a bony grey nag and put a pannier on it for a saddle. As he left, his mother gave him words of advice. Go to Arthur's court, she said. Peredur copied all the horse-trappings he had seen with twisted branches and set off with a fistful of darts. He saw a maiden sitting near the open door of a pavilion and went in. She let him eat half her food and wine; he took a golden ring and left. When the knight who owned the pavilion returned he accused her of sleeping with Peredur and vowed revenge.

Before Peredur reached Arthur's court another knight arrived and insulted Gwenhwyfar by pouring drink over her face and breast. He kept the goblet and left asking someone to follow and fight him for it. All the knights hung their heads, but then Peredur arrived. Cai, a tall man, was standing in the middle of the floor and laughed at Peredur's horse and weapons. He told Peredur to go and get the goblet back. Peredur did so, putting a holly stick through the knight's eye. He left court, swearing loyalty to Arthur and revenge on Cai. That same week he met sixteen knights and overthrew them all. Finally he came to a fortress where a man who said he was his uncle offered to teach him to be a knight.

Peredur went on and came to a great, ivy-covered fortress where a lad with yellow hair leaned over the battlements. In the house he saw a maiden wearing an old dress of silk that showed her white flesh; her hair was blacker than jet and her cheeks red. She gave him a place to sleep, and for three weeks he helped

her overthrow her oppressors. Then he came to a
castle but was told the nine witches of Caerloyw
lived there. At dawn he heard a scream and saw a
witch attacking the watchman. Peredur struck her
head with a sword until her helmet spread out like a
dish. He left and stayed the night in a hermit's cell.
The next morning he found it had snowed and a
wild hawk had killed a duck near the cell. The
hawk rose and a raven descended and Peredur
stood and compared the blackness of the raven and
the whiteness of the snow and the redness of the
blood to the woman he loved best.

Meanwhile Arthur and his retinue were searching
for him. Cai called to him and Peredur struck him,
before Gwalchmai spoke kindly to him and brought
him to Arthur. At the court he met Angharad Law
Eurog and loved her, but she did not love him and he
swore to speak to no Christian until she did. He left,
continuing his journey, killing knights and oppressors, a lion and a serpent until he came back to the
court and found Angharad now loved him.

Arthur went hunting with Peredur and Peredur's

berated Peredur for all the killing he had caused. He set out on a quest for the Fortress of Wonders, until he found that it was the witches of Caerloyw who had been tormenting him. Peredur and Gwalchmai called for Arthur, and he and his retinue attacked the witches and killed them. And that is what is told of the Fortress of Wonders.

Synopsis by Penny Thomas

for the full story see *The Mabinogion, A New Translation* by Sioned Davies (Oxford World's Classics, 2007).

# Afterword

There's no academic basis for this, but Peredur comes across to me as a story written down before it was ready.

There's something unfinished about the tale – clear, perhaps, when we consider the several versions of it that exist. To me, it seems the story hadn't had time to mature and develop before it was put down. (A child sent out into a changing world before he was quite ready.)

I wonder if the 'questing tale' was newly in fashion, and while the other *Mabinogion* stories had time to grow up and accumulate integrity, Peredur – roguish youth as he is – went ahead as a mishmash of popular motifs and events without the narrative balance that comes with giving a story time.

It's a poor piece of prose. If you compare the language and writing with de Troyes' *Perceval*, there is no contest as to which is the more sophisticated, compelling piece.

But let's remember: these were oral tales. To a degree, pantomime. A sentence like: 'Peredur killed the three men then went to the pavilion' is not 'good' writing to read. But performed, how much more would a storyteller have given the line? As Steinbeck pointed out while working on his retelling of Malory's *Morte d'Arthur:* 'The teller of the story could inform his audience with a raised eyebrow or a wink...'

I wanted to keep these two key things when I worked on this book: the unfinished feel of a 'work in progress'; and the idea of performance and exaggeration. The notion that a narrator could put on different hats.

I also wanted to preserve an element of quest. Throughout *Bird, Blood, Snow* there are relics from other books, there for the reader errant to uncover should they wish. Some are somewhat buried, have a patina – they'd need a dusting off. Others lie about on the floor of the text pretty much intact. But it's as you wish. Take it up or not.

As for everything meaning something else, you can take that for granted.

Usually I do the work for a story in my head, then write like I'm remembering. And I try to be clear and precise and economic; and I try to make sure that what my characters do is what they would really do. It wasn't that way here. The task was to cut a shape out of an existing block of someone else's authorship. I enjoyed that. The work happened in a blur. There are clichés, embellishments, anachronisms, but that felt right. I think it's the better for not sanding it smooth.

Cynan Jones

# Acknowledgements

Thanks to Seren for offering me this, and particularly to Penny Thomas. It was a chance to go at something differently.

Thanks also to Sioned Davies for her translation of *The Mabinogion*, which was my central text.

# Appendix

From *The Celtic Echo*

## Multiple Dead Sheep Fuel Big Cat Theory

The discovery locally of an unusual number of dead sheep in the remote hillsides has led to a fear that a big cat could be on the loose.

They were found by a walker, Mr Winton, while on a hike and because the injuries caused to the sheep were so severe some people believe that a big cat is in the area.

Mr Winton, 43, said he'd been walking an old bridleway with his partner Julia, 40, and about two miles off the road heading into the hills they spotted the first dead sheep.

'As we went further, we came across another and it really looked like it had been attacked by something,' he said. 'There must have been seven or eight in the end.

'I wouldn't like to say it was a big cat, but having shown the photos to some friends who work in farming, it seems there are too many for it to be a fox or a dog.

'Of course I'd heard of big cats on the loose before, and I looked for footprints, but couldn't see anything unusual there,' added Mr Winton.

In the 1960s and '70s, it was not unusual for the rich to own a big cat such as a puma or a leopard.

But the Dangerous Animals Act 1976 made it illegal without an expensive license, and it is widely believed that many were simply released into remote areas of wilderness such as Bodmin Moor.

Famously, there is the 'Beast of Bont' legend which first gained prominence after twelve sheep were found mutilated in Ysbyty Ystwyth in 1981, not far from the village of Pontrhydfendigiad in Mid Wales.

There continued to be sporadic sightings and reports of alleged big cat activity in Borth, Talybont, Talgarreg and Bontgoch over recent years and in 1995, 50 sheep were reported to be killed in Pont-rhydfendigiad.

Wild cats such as puma or panthers can live up to fifteen years in the wild and their territories can cover up to 386 square miles.

But a spokesman for the Big Cat Society said: 'From the pictures it is impossible to tell what killed the sheep. But it does not sound like the work of a big cat.

'They kill for food, not usually randomly. In my view at a quick glance there is something other than a big cat at work here, and they would have been also ravaged by scavengers, foxes, birds etc.'

He added: 'Some look a lot older than ten days. Also with that amount of kills something took a long time to kill them.'

A local sheep farmer and NFU spokesman said after looking at Mr Winton's photos: 'There is a difference between a dead sheep and a killed sheep.

And these are killed sheep.'

He was unable to determine what might have caused the animals' death, but he did comment that they looked unusually mutilated.

'Whatever it was it is not something like I have seen before.

'Just from the photos it is clear that whatever it was that did this is certainly a very dangerous and very capable and very violent thing.'

# GWYNETH LEWIS
# THE MEAT TREE

A dangerous tale of desire, DNA, incest and flowers plays out within the wreckage of an ancient spaceship in *The Meat Tree*, an absorbing retelling of one of the best-known Welsh myths by prizewinning writer and poet, Gwyneth Lewis.

An elderly investigator and his female apprentice hope to extract the fate of the ship's crew from its antiquated virtual reality game system, but their empirical approach falters as the story tangles with their own imagination.

By imposing a distance of another 200 years and millions of light years between the reader and the medieval myth, Gwyneth Lewis brings the magical tale of Blodeuwedd, a woman made of flowers, closer than ever before: maybe uncomfortably so.

After all, what man has any idea how sap burns in the veins of a woman?

Gwyneth Lewis was the first National Poet of Wales, 2005-6. She has published seven books of poetry in Welsh and English, the most recent of which is *A Hospital Odyssey*. *Parables and Faxes* won the Aldeburgh Poetry Prize and was also shortlisted for the Forward, as was *Zero Gravity*. Her non-fiction books are *Sunbathing in the Rain: A Cheerful Book on Depression* (shortlisted for the Mind Book of the Year) and *Two in a Boat: A Marital Voyage*.

# OWEN SHEERS
# WHITE RAVENS

"Hauntingly imaginative..." – Dannie Abse

Two stories, two different times, but the thread of an ancient tale runs through the lives of twenty-first-century farmer's daughter Rhian and the mysterious Branwen... Wounded in Italy, Matthew O'Connell is seeing out WWII in a secret government department spreading rumours and myths to the enemy. But when he's given the bizarre task of escorting a box containing six raven chicks from a remote hill farm in Wales to the Tower of London, he becomes part of a story over which he seems to have no control.

Based on the Mabinogion story 'Branwen, Daughter of Llyr', *White Ravens* is a haunting novella from an award-winning writer.

Owen Sheers is the author of two poetry collections, *The Blue Book* and *Skirrid Hill* (both Seren); a Zimbabwean travel narrative, *The Dust Diaries* (Welsh Book of the Year 2005); and a novel, *Resistance*, shortlisted for the Writers' Guild Best Book Award. *A Poet's Guide to Britain* is the accompanying anthology to Owen's BBC 4 series.

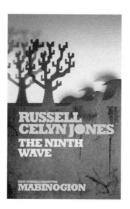

# RUSSELL CELYN JONES
# THE NINTH WAVE

"A brilliantly-imagined vision of the near future...
one of his finest achievements." – Jonathan Coe

Pwyll, a young Welsh ruler in a post-oil world, finds his inherited status hard to take. And he's never quite sure how he's drawn into murdering his future wife's fiancé, losing his only son and switching beds with the king of the underworld. In this bizarrely upside-down, medieval world of the near future, life is cheap and the surf is amazing; but you need a horse to get home again down the M4.

Based on the Mabinogion story 'Pwyll, Lord of Dyfed', *The Ninth Wave* is an eerie and compelling mix of past, present and future. Russell Celyn Jones swops the magical for the psychological, the courtly for the post-feminist and goes back to Swansea Bay to complete some unfinished business.

Russell Celyn Jones is the author of six novels. He has won the David Higham Prize, the Society of Authors Award, and the Weishanhu Award (China). He is a regular reviewer for several national newspapers and is Professor of Creative Writing at Birkbeck College, London.

# NIALL GRIFFITHS
# THE DREAMS OF MAX & RONNIE

There's war and carnage abroad and Iraq-bound squaddie Ronnie is out with his mates 'forgetting what has yet to happen'. He takes something dodgy and falls asleep for three nights in a filthy hovel where he has the strangest of dreams, watching the tattooed tribes of modern Britain surrounding a grinning man playing war games.

Meanwhile gangsta Max is fed up with life in his favourite Cardiff nightclub, Rome, and chases a vision of the perfect woman in far-flung parts of his country. But as Max loses his heart, his followers fear he may be losing his touch.

Niall Griffiths' retellings of two dream myths from the medieval Welsh Mabinogion cycle reveal an astonishingly contemporary and satirical resonance. Arthurian legend merges with its twenty-first century counterpart in a biting commentary on leadership, conflict and the divisions in British society.

Niall Griffiths was born in Liverpool in 1966, studied English, and now lives and works in Aberystwyth. His novels include *Grits, Sheepshagger, Kelly and Victor* and *Stump*, which won Wales Book of the Year, and *Runt*. His non-fiction includes *Real Aberystwyth* and *Real Liverpool*. He also writes reviews, radio plays and travel pieces.

# HORATIO CLARE
# THE PRINCE'S PEN

The Invaders' drones hear all and see all, and England is now a defeated archipelago, but somewhere in the high ground of the far west, insurrection is brewing.

Ludo and Levello, the bandit kings of Wales, call themselves freedom fighters. Levello has the heart and help of Uzma, from Pakistan – the only other country in the free world. Ludo has a secret, lethal if revealed.

Award-winning author Horatio Clare refracts politics, faith and the contemporary world order through the prism of one of the earliest British myths, the Mabinogion, to ask who are the outsiders, who the infidels and who the enemy within...

Horatio Clare is a writer, radio producer and journalist. Born in London, he grew up on a hill farm in the Black Mountains of South Wales as described in his first book *Running for the Hills*, nominated for the *Guardian* First Book Award and shortlisted for the *Sunday Times* Young Writer of the Year Award. Horatio has written about Ethiopia, Namibia and Morocco, and now divides his time between South Wales, Lancashire and London. His other books include *Sicily through Writers' Eyes*, *Truant: Notes from the Slippery Slope* and *A Single Swallow* for which he was the recipient of a Somerset Maugham Award.

# FFLUR DAFYDD
# THE WHITE TRAIL

Life is tough for Cilydd after his heavily pregnant wife vanishes in a supermarket one wintry afternoon. And his private-eye cousin Arthur doesn't appear to be helping much.

The trail leads them to a pigsty, a cliff edge and a bloody warning that Cilydd must never marry again. But eventually the unlikely hero finds himself on a new and dangerous quest – a hunt for the son he never knew, a meeting with a beautiful and mysterious girl, and a glimpse inside the House of the Missing.

In this contemporary retelling from Seren's New Stories from the Mabinogion series, award-winning writer Fflur Dafydd transforms the medieval Welsh Arthurian myth of Culhwch and Olwen into a twenty-first-century quest for love and revenge.

Fflur Dafydd is the author of four novels and one short story collection. She won the Oxfam Hay Emerging Writer of the Year Award 2009 and is the first female author ever to have won both the Prose Medal and the Daniel Owen Memorial Prize at the National Eisteddfod. She has also released three albums as a singer-songwriter and was named BBC Radio Cymru Female Artist of the Year in 2010. She lectures in Creative Writing at Swansea University and lives in Carmarthen with her husband and daughter.